W9-BUE-263

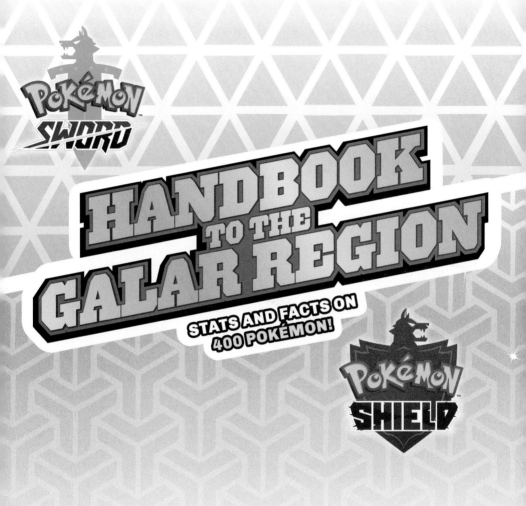

POKÉMON SWORD

HANDBOOK TO THE GALAR REGION

STATS AND FACTS ON 400 POKÉMON!

POKÉMON SHIELD

SCHOLASTIC INC.

All rights reserved. Published by Scholastic Inc., *Publishers since 1920*. SCHOLASTIC and associated logos are trademarks and/or registered trademarks of Scholastic Inc.

The publisher does not have any control over and does not assume any responsibility for author or third-party websites or their content.

ISBN 978-1-338-59252-8

10 9 8 7 6   21 22 23 24

Printed in U.S.A.   40
First printing 2020
Designed by Cheung Tai and Kay Petronio

CONTENTS

Meet the Galar Pokémon!

Welcome to the Galar region!

There's so much to explore in this exciting new region! You'll meet tons of new Pokémon, find new forms of Pokémon you've encountered before, and learn about new skills many familiar Pokémon have developed.

Pokémon play a huge role in the Galar region, and Pokémon battles are very popular. The key to success with Pokémon is staying informed. Information about each Pokémon's type, height, and weight, can make all the difference in raising, battling, and evolving your Pokémon.

In this book, you'll get all the stats and facts you need about the Pokémon of Galar. You'll find out how each Pokémon evolves, what its ability and weaknesses are, which Pokémon have the potential to Gigantamax, and more!

Your mission:

Collect and train as many Pokémon as you can!

You'll start your journey by choosing one of three Pokémon . . .

GROOKEY   SCORBUNNY   SOBBLE

Once you have your first Pokémon, you can catch other Pokémon—and battle other Pokémon!

So get ready, Trainers. Soon you'll be ready to master almost any Pokémon challenge! To keep learning, just turn the page . . .

What are Pokémon?

Pokémon are creatures that come in all shapes, sizes, and personalities.

They live in many types of areas, from oceans and rivers, to mountains and caves, to forests and fields, and more. Trainers can find, capture, train, trade, collect, and use Pokémon in battle against rivals in the quest to become top Pokémon Trainers.

This book contains 400 known species of Pokémon. For most species, there are many individual Pokémon, and some, like Wooloo, even live in herds. Others, like Zacian and Zamazenta, are classified as Legendary Pokémon.

Each individual Pokémon has its own personality. For example, there are a lot of Pikachu, but a Trainer might have a very special one that he or she is pals with.

A Trainer's goal is to befriend and catch Pokémon in the wild and then train them to battle one another. Pokémon do not get seriously hurt in battle. If they are defeated, they faint and then return to the Poké Balls to rest and be healed. A Trainer's job is to take good care of his or her Pokémon.

How to Use This Book

This book will provide the basic stats and facts you need to know to start your Pokémon journey. Here's what you'll discover about each Pokémon:

NAME

TYPE

Each Pokémon has a type, and some even have two! (Pokémon with two types are called dual-type Pokémon.) Every Pokémon type comes with advantages and disadvantages.

CATEGORY

All Pokémon belong to a certain species category.

HOW TO SAY IT

When it comes to Pokémon pronunciation, it's easy to get tongue-tied! There are many Pokémon with unusual names, so we'll help you sound them out. Soon you'll be saying Pokémon names so perfectly, you'll sound like a professor!

HEIGHT AND WEIGHT

How does each Pokémon measure up? Find out by checking its height and weight stats. And remember, good things come in all shapes and sizes. It's up to every Trainer to work with his or her Pokémon and play up its strengths.

GENDER

Most Pokémon are both male (♂) and female (♀,) but some are exclusively one gender or have an unknown gender.

ABILITY

Each Pokémon has an Ability that can help it in battle. A Pokémon's Ability usually relates back to its type in one way or another. Some Pokémon have one of two possible Abilities.

WEAKNESSES

In a battle, the effectiveness of a Pokémon's moves depends on the type of its opponent. A Pokémon's weaknesses show what other types will most successfully be able to damage it in an attack!

EVOLUTION

If your Pokémon has an evolved form or pre-evolved form, we'll show you its place in the chain and how it evolves.

DESCRIPTION

Knowledge is power! Pokémon Trainers have to know their stuff. Find out everything you need to know about your Pokémon here.

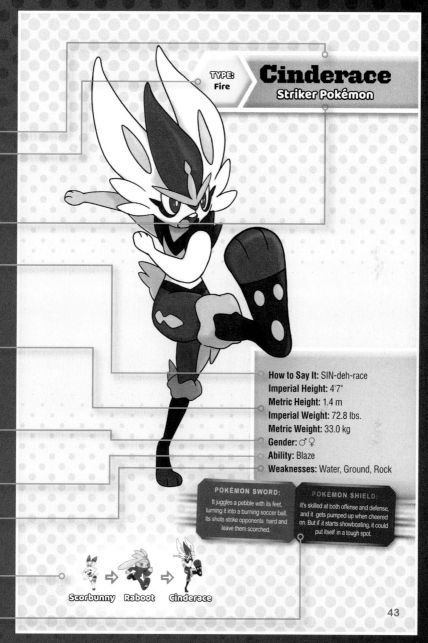

TYPE: Fire

Cinderace
Striker Pokémon

How to Say It: SIN-deh-race
Imperial Height: 4'7"
Metric Height: 1.4 m
Imperial Weight: 72.8 lbs.
Metric Weight: 33.0 kg
Gender: ♂ ♀
Ability: Blaze
Weaknesses: Water, Ground, Rock

POKÉMON SWORD:
It juggles a pebble with its feet, turning it into a burning soccer ball. Its shots strike opponents hard and leave them scorched.

POKÉMON SHIELD:
It's skilled at both offense and defense, and it gets pumped up when cheered on. But if it starts showboating, it could put itself in a tough spot.

Scorbunny ⇨ Raboot ⇨ Cinderace

43

GIGANTAMAX POKÉMON

In the Galar region, some Pokémon have a Gigantamax form. It's a special kind of Dynamax that both increases their size and changes their appearance! Gigantamax Pokémon are extremely rare—not every Pokémon of a given species can Gigantamax—and each has access to a special G-Max Move.

Guide to Pokémon Types

Type is the key to unlocking a Pokémon's power.

A Pokémon's type can tell you a lot about it—from where to find it in the wild to the moves it will be able to use on the battlefield. For example, Water-type Pokémon usually live in lakes, rivers, and oceans.

A clever Trainer should always consider type when picking a Pokémon for a match, because type shows a Pokémon's strengths and weaknesses. For example, a Fire type may melt an Ice type, but against a Water type, it might find *it's* the one in hot water. And while a Water type usually has the upper hand in battle with a Fire type, a Water-type move would act like a sprinkler on a Grass-type Pokémon. But when that same Grass type is battling a Fire type, it just might get scorched.

BUG

GRASS

DARK

GROUND

DRAGON

ICE

ELECTRIC

NORMAL

FAIRY

POISON

FIGHTING

PSYCHIC

FIRE

ROCK

FLYING

STEEL

GHOST

WATER

Battle Basics

WHY BATTLE?

There are two basic reasons for a Pokémon to battle. One is for sport. You can battle another Trainer in a friendly competition. Your Pokémon do the fighting, but you decide which Pokémon and which moves to use.

The second reason is to catch wild Pokémon. Wild Pokémon have no training and no owners. They can be found pretty much anywhere. Battle is one of the main ways to catch a Pokémon. But other Trainers' Pokémon are off-limits. You can't capture their Pokémon, even if you win a competition.

WHICH POKÉMON TO USE?

As you prepare for your first battle, you may have several Pokémon to choose from. Use the resources in this book to help you decide which Pokémon would be best. If you're facing a Fire type like Scorbunny, you can put out its sparks with a Water type like Sobble.

THE FACE-OFF

You and your Pokémon will have to face and hopefully defeat each and every Pokémon on the other Trainer's team. You win when your Pokémon have defeated all the other Trainer's Pokémon. A Pokémon is defeated when it gets so weak it faints.

POKÉMON STATS AND FACTS

Ready to discover more about each Pokémon? Turn the page and begin!

Abomasnow

Frost Tree Pokémon

TYPE:
Grass-Ice

How to Say It: ah-BOM-ah-snow
Imperial Height: 7'3"
Metric Height: 2.2 m
Imperial Weight: 298.7 lbs.
Metric Weight: 135.5 kg
Gender: ♂♀
Ability: Snow Warning
Weaknesses: Fire, Bug, Fighting, Flying, Poison, Rock, Steel

POKÉMON SWORD:
If it sees any packs of Darumaka going after Snover, it chases them off, swinging its sizable arms like hammers.

POKÉMON SHIELD:
This Pokémon is known to bring blizzards. A shake of its massive body is enough to cause whiteout conditions.

Snover   Abomasnow

Accelgor

Shell Out Pokémon

TYPE:
Bug

How to Say It: ak-SELL-gohr
Imperial Height: 2'7"
Metric Height: 0.8 m
Imperial Weight: 55.8 lbs.
Metric Weight: 25.3 kg
Gender: ♂♀
Ability: Hydration / Sticky Hold
Weaknesses: Fire, Flying, Rock

POKÉMON SWORD:
It moves with blinding speed and lobs poison at foes. Featuring Accelgor as a main character is a surefire way to make a movie or comic popular.

POKÉMON SHIELD:
Discarding its shell made it nimble. To keep itself from dehydrating, it wraps its body in bands of membrane.

Shelmet   Accelgor

Aegislash
Royal Sword Pokémon

How to Say It: EE-jih-SLASH
Imperial Height: 5'7"
Metric Height: 1.7 m
Imperial Weight: 116.8 lbs.
Metric Weight: 53.0 kg
Gender: ♂ ♀
Ability: Stance Change
Weaknesses: Fire, Ghost, Dark, Ground

Blade Form

POKÉMON SWORD:
In this defensive stance, Aegislash uses its steel body and a force field of spectral power to reduce the damage of any attack.

POKÉMON SHIELD:
Its potent spectral powers allow it to manipulate others. It once used its powers to force people and Pokémon to build a kingdom to its liking.

Honedge ⇨ Doublade ⇨ Aegislash

15

Alcremie

Cream Pokémon

How to Say It: AL-kruh-mee
Imperial Height: 1'
Metric Height: 0.3 m
Imperial Weight: 1.1 lbs.
Metric Weight: 0.5 kg
Gender: ♀
Ability: Sweet Veil
Weaknesses: Steel, Poison

POKÉMON SWORD:
When it trusts a Trainer, it will treat them to berries it's decorated with cream.

POKÉMON SHIELD:
When Alcremie is content, the cream it secretes from its hands becomes sweeter and richer.

Milcery ⇨ Alcremie

Gigantamax Alcremie

Imperial Height: 98'5"+
Metric Height: 30.0+ m
Imperial Weight: ?????.? lbs.
Metric Weight: ?????.? kg

POKÉMON SWORD:
When it trusts a Trainer, it will treat them to berries it's decorated with cream.

POKÉMON SHIELD:
When Alcremie is content, the cream it secretes from its hands becomes sweeter and richer.

Appletun
Apple Nectar Pokémon

How to Say It: AP-pell-tun
Imperial Height: 1'4"
Metric Height: 0.4 m
Imperial Weight: 28.7 lbs.
Metric Weight: 13.0 kg
Gender: ♂ ♀
Ability: Ripen / Gluttony
Weaknesses: Flying, Ice, Dragon,
Poison, Fairy, Bug

POKÉMON SWORD:
Eating a sweet apple caused its evolution. A nectarous scent wafts from its body, luring in the bug Pokémon it preys on

POKEMON SHIELD:
Its body is covered in sweet nectar, and the skin on its back is especially yummy. Children used to have it as a snack.

Appletun

Flapple

Applin

Gigantamax Appletun

Imperial Height: 78'9"+
Metric Height: 24.0+ m
Imperial Weight: ?????.? lbs.
Metric Weight: ?????.? kg

POKÉMON SWORD:
It blasts its opponents with massive amounts of sweet, sticky nectar, drowning them under the deluge.

POKÉMON SHIELD:
Due to Gigantamax energy, this Pokémon's nectar has thickened. The increased viscosity lets the nectar absorb more damage than before.

Applin
Apple Core Pokémon

How to Say It: AP-lin
Imperial Height: 8"
Metric Height: .2 m
Imperial Weight: 1.1 lbs.
Metric Weight: 0.5 kg
Gender: ♂ ♀
Ability: Ripen / Gluttony
Weaknesses: Flying, Ice, Dragon, Poison, Fairy, Bug

POKÉMON SWORD:
It spends its entire life inside an apple. It hides from its natural enemies, bird Pokémon, by pretending it's just an apple and nothing more.

POKÉMON SHIELD:
As soon as it's born, it burrows into an apple. Not only does the apple serve as its food source, but the flavor of the fruit determines its evolution.

Applin Appletun Flapple

Araquanid
Water Bubble Pokémon

How to Say It: uh-RACK-wuh-nid
Imperial Height: 5'11"
Metric Height: 1.8 m
Imperial Weight: 180.8 lbs.
Metric Weight: 82.0 kg
Gender: ♂ ♀
Ability: Water Bubble
Weaknesses: Flying, Electric, Rock

POKÉMON SWORD:
It launches water bubbles with its legs, drowning prey within the bubbles. This Pokémon can then take its time to savor its meal.

POKÉMON SHIELD:
It acts as a caretaker for Dewpider, putting them inside its bubble and letting them eat any leftover food.

Dewpider Araquanid

Arcanine

Legendary Pokémon

How to Say It: ARE-ka-nine
Imperial Height: 6'3"
Metric Height: 1.9 m
Imperial Weight: 341.7 lbs.
Metric Weight: 155.0 kg
Gender: ♂ ♀
Ability: Intimidate / Flash Fire
Weaknesses: Ground, Rock, Water

POKÉMON SWORD:
The sight of it running over 6,200 miles in a single day and night has captivated many people.

POKÉMON SHIELD:
A Pokémon that has long been admired for its beauty. It runs agilely, as if on wings.

 ⇨

Growlithe   Arcanine

Arctovish

Fossil Pokémon

TYPE:
Water-
Ice

How to Say It: ARK-toh-vish
Imperial Height: 6'7"
Metric Height: 2.0 m
Imperial Weight: 385.8 lbs.
Metric Weight: 175.0 kg
Gender: Unknown
Ability: Water Absorb / Ice Body
Weaknesses: Grass, Electric, Fighting, Rock

POKÉMON SWORD:
Though it's able to capture prey by freezing its surroundings, it has trouble eating the prey afterward because its mouth is on top of its head.

POKÉMON SHIELD:
The skin on its face is impervious to attack, but breathing difficulties made this Pokémon go extinct anyway.

Does not evolve.

Arctozolt

Fossil Pokémon

TYPE:
Electric-Ice

How to Say It: ARK-toh-zohlt
Imperial Height: 7'7"
Metric Height: 2.3 m
Imperial Weight: 330.7 lbs.
Metric Weight: 150.0 kg
Gender: Unknown
Ability: Volt Absorb / Static
Weaknesses: Fire, Ground, Fighting, Rock

POKÉMON SWORD:
The shaking of its freezing upper half is what generates its electricity. It has a hard time walking around.

POKÉMON SHIELD:
This Pokémon lived on prehistoric seashores and was able to preserve food with the ice on its body. It went extinct because it moved so slowly.

Does not evolve

Aromatisse

Fragrance Pokémon

TYPE: Fairy

How to Say It: uh-ROME-uh-teece
Imperial Height: 2'7"
Metric Height: 0.8 m
Imperial Weight: 34.2 lbs.
Metric Weight: 15.5 kg
Gender: ♂ ♀
Ability: Healer
Weaknesses: Steel, Poison

POKÉMON SWORD:
The scent that constantly emits from its fur is so powerful that this Pokémon's companions will eventually lose their sense of smell.

POKÉMON SHIELD:
The scents Aromatisse can produce range from sweet smells that bolster allies to foul smells that sap an opponent's will to fight.

Spritzee ⇨ **Aromatisse**

TYPE: Water

Arrokuda

Rush Pokémon

How to Say It: AIR-oh-KOO-duh
Imperial Height: 1'8"
Metric Height: 0.5 m
Imperial Weight: 2.2 lbs.
Metric Weight: 1.0 kg
Gender: ♂ ♀
Ability: Swift Swim
Weaknesses: Grass, Electric

POKÉMON SWORD:
If it sees any movement around it, this Pokémon charges for it straightaway, leading with its sharply pointed jaw. It's very proud of that jaw.

POKÉMON SHIELD:
After it's eaten its fill, its movements become extremely sluggish. That's when Cramorant swallows it up.

Arrokuda ⇨ **Barraskewda**

Avalugg
Iceberg Pokémon

How to Say It: AV-uh-lug
Imperial Height: 6'7"
Metric Height: 2.0 m
Imperial Weight: 1113.3 lbs.
Metric Weight: 505.0 kg
Gender: ♂ ♀
Ability: Own Tempo / Ice Body
Weaknesses: Fire, Steel, Fighting, Rock

POKÉMON SWORD:
At high latitudes, this Pokémon can be found with clusters of Bergmite on its back as it swims among the icebergs.

POKÉMON SHIELD:
As Avalugg moves about during the day, the cracks in its body deepen. The Pokémon's body returns to a pristine state overnight.

Bergmite   Avalugg

Axew
Tusk Pokémon

TYPE: Dragon

How to Say It: AKS-yoo
Imperial Height: 2'
Metric Height: 0.6 m
Imperial Weight: 39.7 lbs.
Metric Weight: 18.0 kg
Gender: ♂ ♀
Ability: Rivalry / Mold Breaker
Weaknesses: Ice, Dragon, Fairy

POKÉMON SWORD:
These Pokémon nest in the ground and use their tusks to crush hard berries. Crushing berries is also how they test each other's strength.

POKÉMON SHIELD:
They play with each other by knockin their large tusks together. Their tusk break sometimes, but they grow bac so quickly that it isn't a concern.

Axew   Fraxure   Haxorus

Baltoy
Clay Doll Pokémon

TYPE:
Ground-Psychic

How to Say It: BAL-toy
Imperial Height: 1'8"
Metric Height: 0.5 m
Imperial Weight: 47.4 lbs.
Metric Weight: 21.5 kg
Gender: Unknown
Ability: Levitate
Weaknesses: Bug, Dark, Ghost, Grass, Water, Ice

POKÉMON SWORD:
It moves while spinning around on its single foot. Some Baltoy have been seen spinning on their heads.

POKÉMON SHIELD:
It was discovered in ancient ruins. While moving, it constantly spins. It stands on one foot even when asleep.

Baltoy ⇨ **Claydol**

Barbaracle
Collective Pokémon

TYPE:
Rock-Water

How to Say It: bar-BARE-uh-kull
Imperial Height: 4'3"
Metric Height: 1.3 m
Imperial Weight: 211.6 lbs.
Metric Weight: 96.0 kg
Gender: ♂♀
Ability: Tough Claws / Sniper
Weaknesses: Electric, Fighting, Grass, Ground

POKÉMON SWORD:
Seven Binacle come together to form one Barbaracle. The Binacle that serves as the head gives orders to those serving as the limbs.

POKÉMON SHIELD:
Having an eye on each palm allows it to keep watch in all directions. In a pinch, its limbs start to act on their own to ensure the enemy's defeat.

Binacle ⇨ **Barbaracle**

Barboach
Whiskers Pokémon

TYPE:
Water-Ground

How to Say It: bar-BOACH
Imperial Height: 1'4"
Metric Height: 0.4 m
Imperial Weight: 4.2 lbs.
Metric Weight: 1.9 kg
Gender: ♂♀
Ability: Oblivious / Anticipation
Weaknesses: Grass

POKÉMON SWORD:
Its slimy body is hard to grasp. In one region, it is said to have been born from hardened mud.

POKÉMON SHIELD:
It probes muddy riverbeds with its two long whiskers. A slimy film protects its body.

Barboach ⇨ **Whiscash**

TYPE:
Water

Barraskewda
Skewer Pokémon

How to Say It: BAIR-uh-SKYOO-duh
Imperial Height: 4'3"
Metric Height: 1.3 m
Imperial Weight: 66.1 lbs.
Metric Weight: 30.0 kg
Gender: ♂♀
Ability: Swift Swim
Weaknesses: Grass, Electric

POKÉMON SWORD:
This Pokémon has a jaw that's as sharp as a spear and as strong as steel. Apparently Barraskewda's flesh is surprisingly tasty, too.

POKÉMON SHIELD:
It spins its tail fins to propel itself, surging forward at speeds of over 100 knots before ramming prey and spearing into them.

Arrokuda ⇨ **Barraskewda**

Basculin
Hostile Pokémon

TYPE:
Water

Red-Striped Form

Blue-Striped Form

How to Say It: BASS-kyoo-lin
Imperial Height: 3'3"
Metric Height: 1.0 m
Imperial Weight: 39.7 lbs.
Metric Weight: 18.0 kg
Gender: ♂♀ (Red-Striped Form); Unknown (Blue-Striped Form)
Ability: Adaptability / Reckless (Red-Striped Form) / Rock Head (Blue-Striped Form)
Weaknesses: Grass, Electric

RED-STRIPED FORM

POKÉMON SWORD:
Anglers love the fight this Pokémon puts up on the hook. And there are always more to catch—many people release them into lakes illicitly.

POKÉMON SHIELD:
In the past, it often appeared on the dinner table. The meat of red-striped Basculin is on the fatty side, and it's more popular with the youth.

BLUE-STRIPED FORM

POKÉMON SWORD:
Blue-striped Basculin used to be a common food source. They apparently have an inoffensive, light flavor.

POKÉMON SHIELD:
Known for their violence, these Pokémon have the most fights with schools of red-striped Basculin.

Does not evolve.

TYPE:
Ice

Beartic
Freezing Pokémon

How to Say It: BAIR-tick
Imperial Height: 8'6"
Metric Height: 2.6 m
Imperial Weight: 573.2 lbs.
Metric Weight: 260.0 kg
Gender: ♂♀
Ability: Snow Cloak / Slush Rush
Weaknesses: Fire, Fighting, Rock, Steel

POKÉMON SWORD:
It swims through frigid seas, searching for prey. From its frozen breath, it forms icy fangs that are harder than steel.

POKÉMON SHIELD:
It swims energetically through frigid seas. When it gets tired, it freezes the seawater with its breath so it can rest on the ice.

Cubchoo ⇨ **Beartic**

Beheeyem
Cerebral Pokémon

How to Say It: BEE-hee-ehm
Imperial Height: 3'3"
Metric Height: 1.0 m
Imperial Weight: 76.1 lbs.
Metric Weight: 34.5 kg
Gender: ♂ ♀
Ability: Synchronize / Telepathy
Weaknesses: Bug, Ghost, Dark

POKÉMON SWORD:
Whenever a Beheeyem visits a farm, a Dubwool mysteriously disappears.

POKÉMON SHIELD:
Sometimes found drifting above wheat fields, this Pokémon can control the memories of its opponents.

Elgyem ➪ Beheeyem

Bellossom
Flower Pokémon

TYPE:
Grass

How to Say It: bell-LAHS-um
Imperial Height: 1'4"
Metric Height: 0.4 m
Imperial Weight: 12.8 lbs.
Metric Weight: 5.8 kg
Gender: ♂ ♀
Ability: Chlorophyll
Weaknesses: Bug, Fire, Flying, Ice, Poison

POKÉMON SWORD:
Plentiful in the tropics. When it dances, its petals rub together and make a pleasant ringing sound.

POKÉMON SHIELD:
Bellossom gather at times and appear to dance. They say that the dance is a ritual to summon the sun.

  Vileplume

Oddish Gloom

Bellossom

Bergmite

Ice Chunk Pokémon

TYPE:
Ice

How to Say It: BERG-mite
Imperial Height: 3'3"
Metric Height: 1.0 m
Imperial Weight: 219.4 lbs.
Metric Weight: 99.5 kg
Gender: ♂ ♀
Ability: Own Tempo / Ice Body
Weaknesses: Fire, Steel, Fighting, Rock

POKÉMON SWORD:
They chill the air around them to −150 degrees Fahrenheit, freezing the water in the air into ice that they use as armor.

POKÉMON SHIELD:
This Pokémon lives in areas of frigid cold. It secures itself to the back of an Avalugg by freezing its feet in place.

Bergmite **Avalugg**

Bewear

Strong Arm Pokémon

TYPE:
Normal-
Fighting

How to Say It: beh-WARE
Imperial Height: 6'11"
Metric Height: 2.1 m
Imperial Weight: 297.6 lbs.
Metric Weight: 135.0 kg
Gender: ♂ ♀
Ability: Fluffy / Klutz
Weaknesses: Psychic, Flying, Fairy, Fighting

POKÉMON SWORD:
Once it accepts you as a friend, it tries to show its affection with a hug. Letting it do that is dangerous—it could easily shatter your bones.

POKÉMON SHIELD:
The moves it uses to take down its prey would make a martial artist jealous. It tucks subdued prey under its arms to carry them to its nest.

Stufful   **Bewear**

Binacle
Two-Handed Pokémon

TYPE:
Rock-
Water

How to Say It: BY-nuh-kull
Imperial Height: 1'8"
Metric Height: 0.5 m
Imperial Weight: 68.3 lbs.
Metric Weight: 31.0 kg
Gender: ♂♀
Ability: Tough Claws / Sniper
Weaknesses: Electric, Fighting, Grass,
Ground

POKÉMON SWORD:
After two Binacle find a suitably sized rock, they adhere themselves to it and live together. They cooperate to gather food during high tide.

POKÉMON SHIELD:
If the two don't work well together, both their offense and defense fall apart. Without good teamwork, they won't survive.

Binacle   Barbaracle

TYPE:
Dark-
Steel

Bisharp
Sword Blade Pokémon

How to Say It: BIH-sharp
Imperial Height: 5'3"
Metric Height: 1.6 m
Imperial Weight: 154.3 lbs.
Metric Weight: 70.0 kg
Gender: ♂♀
Ability: Defiant / Inner Focus
Weaknesses: Fighting, Fire, Ground

POKÉMON SWORD:
It's accompanied by a large retinue of Pawniard. Bisharp keeps a keen eye on its minions, ensuring none of them even think of double-crossing it.

POKÉMON SHIELD:
Violent conflicts erupt between Bisharp and Fraxure over places where sharpening stones can be found.

Pawniard   Bisharp

Blipbug
Larva Pokémon

How to Say It: BLIP-bug
Imperial Height: 1'4"
Metric Height: 0.4 m
Imperial Weight: 17.6 lbs.
Metric Weight: 8.0 kg
Gender: ♂♀
Ability: Swarm / Compound Eyes
Weaknesses: Fire, Flying, Rock

POKÉMON SWORD:
A constant collector of information, this Pokémon is very smart. Very strong is what it isn't.

POKÉMON SHIELD:
Often found in gardens, this Pokémon has hairs on its body that it uses to assess its surroundings.

Blipbug ⇨ **Dottler** ⇨ **Orbeetle**

TYPE: **Rock**

Boldore
Ore Pokémon

How to Say It: BOHL-dohr
Imperial Height: 2'11"
Metric Height: 0.9 m
Imperial Weight: 224.9 lbs.
Metric Weight: 102.0 kg
Gender: ♂♀
Ability: Sturdy / Weak Armor
Weaknesses: Water, Grass, Fighting, Ground, Steel

POKÉMON SWORD:
If you see its orange crystals start to glow, be wary. It's about to fire off bursts of energy.

POKÉMON SHIELD:
It relies on sound in order to monitor what's in its vicinity. When angered, it will attack without ever changing the direction it's facing.

oggenrola ⇨ **Boldore** ⇨ **Gigalith**

Boltund

Dog Pokémon

How to Say It: BOHL-tund
Imperial Height: 3'3"
Metric Height: 1.0 m
Imperial Weight: 75.0 lbs.
Metric Weight: 34.0 kg
Gender: ♂ ♀
Ability: Strong Jaw
Weaknesses: Ground

POKÉMON SWORD:
This Pokémon generates electricity and channels it into its legs to keep them going strong. Boltund can run nonstop for three full days.

POKÉMON SHIELD:
It sends electricity through its legs to boost their strength. Running at top speed, it easily breaks 50 mph.

Yamper ⇨ **Boltund**

TYPE: Rock

Bonsly

Bonsai Pokémon

How to Say It: BON-slye
Imperial Height: 1'8"
Metric Height: 0.5 m
Imperial Weight: 33.1 lbs.
Metric Weight: 15.0 kg
Gender: ♂ ♀
Ability: Sturdy / Rock Head
Weaknesses: Fighting, Grass, Ground, Steel, Water

POKÉMON SWORD:
It expels both sweat and tears from its eyes. The sweat is a little salty, while the tears have a slight bitterness.

POKÉMON SHIELD:
This Pokémon lives in dry, rocky areas. As its green spheres dry out, their dull luster increases.

Bonsly ⇨ **Sudowoodo**

Bounsweet
Fruit Pokémon

How to Say It: BOWN*-sweet
(*Rhymes with DOWN)
Imperial Height: 1'
Metric Height: 0.3 m
Imperial Weight: 7.1 lbs.
Metric Weight: 3.2 kg
Gender: ♀
Ability: Leaf Guard / Oblivious
Weaknesses: Fire, Flying, Ice, Poison, Bug

POKÉMON SWORD:
Its body gives off a sweet, fruity scent that is extremely appetizing to bird Pokémon.

POKÉMON SHIELD:
When under attack, it secretes a sweet and delicious sweat. The scent only calls more enemies to it.

Bounsweet　Steenee　Tsareena

Braviary
Valiant Pokémon

**TYPE:
Normal-
Flying**

How to Say It: BRAY-vee-air-ee
Imperial Height: 4'11"
Metric Height: 1.5 m
Imperial Weight: 90.4 lbs.
Metric Weight: 41.0 kg
Gender: ♂
Ability: Keen Eye / Sheer Force
Weaknesses: Electric, Ice, Rock

POKÉMON SWORD:
Known for its bravery and pride, this majestic Pokémon is often seen as a motif for various kinds of emblems.

POKÉMON SHIELD:
Because this Pokémon is hotheaded and belligerent, it's Corviknight that's taken the role of transportation in Galar.

Rufflet

Braviary

Bronzong

Bronze Bell Pokémon

How to Say It: brawn-ZONG
Imperial Height: 4'3"
Metric Height: 1.3 m
Imperial Weight: 412.3 lbs.
Metric Weight: 187.0 kg
Gender: Unknown
Ability: Levitate / Heatproof
Weaknesses: Fire, Ground, Ghost, Dark

POKÉMON SWORD:
Some believe it to be a deity that summons rain clouds. When angered, it lets out a warning cry that rings out like the tolling of a bell.

POKÉMON SHIELD:
Many scientists suspect that this Pokémon originated outside the Galar region, based on the patterns on its body.

Bronzor ⇨ Bronzong

Bronzor

Bronze Pokémon

How to Say It: BRAWN-zor
Imperial Height: 1'8"
Metric Height: 0.5 m
Imperial Weight: 133.4 lbs.
Metric Weight: 60.5 kg
Gender: Unknown
Ability: Levitate / Heatproof
Weaknesses: Fire, Ground, Ghost, Dark

POKÉMON SWORD:
It appears in ancient ruins. The pattern on its body doesn't come from any culture in the Galar region, so it remains shrouded in mystery.

POKÉMON SHIELD:
Polishing Bronzor to a shine makes its surface reflect the truth, according to common lore. Be that as it may, Bronzor hates being polished.

Bronzor ⇨ Bronzong

Budew
Bud Pokémon

How to Say It: buh-DEW
Imperial Height: 8"
Metric Height: 0.2 m
Imperial Weight: 2.6 lbs.
Metric Weight: 1.2 kg
Gender: ♂♀
Ability: Natural Cure / Poison Point
Weaknesses: Fire, Flying, Ice, Psychic

POKÉMON SWORD:
The pollen it releases contains poison. If this Pokémon is raised on clean water, the poison's toxicity is increased.

POKÉMON SHIELD:
This Pokémon is highly sensitive to temperature changes. When its bud starts to open, that means spring is right around the corner.

Budew ⇨ Roselia ⇨ Roserade

Bunnelby
Digging Pokémon

How to Say It: BUN-el-bee
Imperial Height: 1'4"
Metric Height: 0.4 m
Imperial Weight: 11.0 lbs.
Metric Weight: 5.0 kg
Gender: ♂♀
Ability: Pickup / Cheek Pouch
Weaknesses: Fighting

POKÉMON SWORD:
It excels at digging holes. Using its ears, it can dig a nest 33 feet deep in one night.

POKÉMON SHIELD:
It's very sensitive to danger. The sound of Corviknight's flapping will have Bunnelby digging a hole to hide underground in moments.

Bunnelby ⇨ Diggersby

Butterfree
Butterfly Pokémon

TYPE:
Bug-Flying

How to Say It: BUT-er-free
Imperial Height: 3'7"
Metric Height: 1.1 m
Imperial Weight: 70.5 lbs.
Metric Weight: 32.0 kg
Gender: ♂ ♀
Ability: Compound Eyes
Weaknesses: Rock, Electric, Fire, Flying, Ice

POKÉMON SWORD:
In battle, it flaps its wings at great speed to release highly toxic dust into the air.

POKÉMON SHIELD:
It collects honey every day. It rubs honey onto the hairs on its legs to carry it back to its nest.

Caterpie ⇨ Metapod ⇨ Butterfree

Gigantamax Butterfree

Imperial Height: 55'9"+
Metric Height: 17.0+ m
Imperial Weight: ????.? lbs.
Metric Weight: ????.? kg

POKÉMON SWORD:
Crystallized Gigantamax energy makes up this Pokémon's blindingly bright and highly toxic scales.

POKÉMON SHIELD:
Once it has opponents trapped in a tornado that could blow away a 10-ton truck, it finishes them off with its poisonous scales.

Carkol
Coal Pokémon

How to Say It: KAR-kohl
Imperial Height: 3'7"
Metric Height: 1.1 m
Imperial Weight: 172.0 lbs.
Metric Weight: 78.0 kg
Gender: ♂ ♀
Ability: Steam Engine / Flame Body
Weaknesses: Water, Ground, Fighting, Rock

POKÉMON SWORD:
It forms coal inside its body. Coal dropped by this Pokémon once helped fuel the lives of people in the Galar region.

POKÉMON SHIELD:
By rapidly rolling its legs, it can travel at over 18 mph. The temperature of the flames it breathes exceeds 1,800 degrees Fahrenheit.

Rolycoly **Carkol** **Coalossal**

Caterpie
Worm Pokémon

TYPE:
Bug

How to Say It: CAT-ur-pee
Imperial Height: 1'
Metric Height: 0.3 m
Imperial Weight: 6.4 lbs.
Metric Weight: 2.9 kg
Gender: ♂ ♀
Ability: Shield Dust
Weaknesses: Fire, Flying, Rock

POKÉMON SWORD:
For protection, it releases a horrible stench from the antenna on its head to drive away enemies.

POKÉMON SHIELD:
Its short feet are tipped with suction pads that enable it to tirelessly climb slopes and walls.

aterpie **Metapod** **Butterfree**

Centiskorch

Radiator Pokémon

How to Say It: SEN-tih-scorch
Imperial Height: 9'10"
Metric Height: 3.0 m
Imperial Weight: 264.4 lbs.
Metric Weight: 120.0 kg
Gender: ♂♀
Ability: Flash Fire / White Smoke
Weaknesses: Water, Flying, Rock

POKÉMON SWORD:
When it heats up, its body temperature reaches about 1,500 degrees Fahrenheit. It lashes its body like a whip and launches itself at enemies.

POKÉMON SHIELD:
While its burning body is already dangerous on its own, this excessively hostile Pokémon also has large and very sharp fangs.

Sizzlipede   Centiskorch

Gigantamax Centiskorch

Imperial Height: 246'1"+
Metric Height: 75.0+ m
Imperial Weight: ?????.? lbs.
Metric Weight: ?????.? kg

POKÉMON SWORD:
Gigantamax energy has evoked a rise in its body temperature, now reaching over 1,800 degrees Fahrenheit. Its heat waves incinerate its enemies.

POKÉMON SHIELD:
The heat that comes off a Gigantamax Centiskorch may destabilize air currents. Sometimes it can even cause storms.

Chandelure
Luring Pokémon

How to Say It: shan-duh-LOOR
Imperial Height: 3'3"
Metric Height: 1.0 m
Imperial Weight: 75.6 lbs.
Metric Weight: 34.3 kg
Gender: ♂ ♀
Ability: Flash Fire / Flame Body
Weaknesses: Water, Ground,
Rock, Ghost, Dark

POKÉMON SWORD:
This Pokémon haunts dilapidated mansions. It sways its arms to hypnotize opponents with the ominous dancing of its flames.

POKÉMON SHIELD:
In homes illuminated by Chandelure instead of lights, funerals were a constant occurrence— or so it's said.

Litwick   Lampent   Chandelure

Charizard

Flame Pokémon

TYPE:
Fire-
Flying

How to Say It: CHAR-iz-ard
Imperial Height: 5'7"
Metric Height: 1.7 m
Imperial Weight: 199.5 lbs.
Metric Weight: 90.5 kg
Gender: ♂ ♀
Ability: Blaze
Weaknesses: Rock, Electric, Water

POKÉMON SWORD:
It spits fire that is hot enough to melt boulders. It may cause forest fires by blowing flames.

POKÉMON SHIELD:
Its wings can carry this Pokémon close to an altitude of 4,600 feet. It blows out fire at very high temperatures.

Charmander ⇨ Charmeleon ⇨ Chariza

Gigantamax Charizard

Imperial Height: 91'10"+
Metric Height: 28.0+ m
Imperial Weight: ?????.? lbs.
Metric Weight: ?????.? kg

POKÉMON SWORD:
This colossal, flame-winged figure of a Charizard was brought about by Gigantamax energy.

POKÉMON SHIELD:
The flame inside its body burns hotter than 3,600 degrees Fahrenheit. When Charizard roars, that temperature climbs even higher.

Charjabug
Battery Pokémon

How to Say It: CHAR-juh-bug
Imperial Height: 1'8"
Metric Height: 0.5 m
Imperial Weight: 23.1 lbs.
Metric Weight: 10.5 kg
Gender: ♂♀
Ability: Battery
Weaknesses: Fire, Rock

POKÉMON SWORD:
While its durable shell protects it from attacks, Charjabug strikes at enemies with jolts of electricity discharged from the tips of its jaws.

POKÉMON SHIELD:
Its digestive processes convert the leaves it eats into electricity. An electric sac in its belly stores the electricity for later use.

Grubbin   Charjabug   Vikavolt

TYPE:
Fire

Charmander
Lizard Pokémon

How to Say It: CHAR-man-der
Imperial Height: 2'
Metric Height: 0.6 m
Imperial Weight: 18.7 lbs.
Metric Weight: 8.5 kg
Gender: ♂♀
Ability: Blaze
Weaknesses: Ground, Rock, Water

POKÉMON SWORD:
It has a preference for hot things. When it rains, steam is said to spout from the tip of its tail.

POKÉMON SHIELD:
From the time it is born, a flame burns at the tip of its tail. Its life would end if the flame were to go out.

armander   Charmeleon   Charizard

Charmeleon
Flame Pokémon

TYPE:
Fire

How to Say It: char-MEE-lee-un
Imperial Height: 3'7"
Metric Height: 1.1 m
Imperial Weight: 41.9 lbs.
Metric Weight: 19.0 kg
Gender: ♂♀
Ability: Blaze
Weaknesses: Ground, Rock, Water

POKÉMON SWORD:
It has a barbaric nature. In battle, it whips its fiery tail around and slashes away with sharp claws.

POKÉMON SHIELD:
If it becomes agitated during battle, it spouts intense flames, incinerating its surroundings.

Charmander   Charmeleon   Chariza

TYPE:
Grass

Cherrim
Blossom Pokémon

Sunshine Form

How to Say It: chuh-RIM
Imperial Height: 1'8"
Metric Height: 0.5 m
Imperial Weight: 20.5 lbs.
Metric Weight: 9.3 kg
Gender: ♂♀
Ability: Flower Gift
Weaknesses: Bug, Fire, Flying, Ice, Poison

POKÉMON SWORD:
As a bud, it barely moves. It sits still, placidly waiting for sunlight to appear.

POKÉMON SHIELD:
Its folded petals are pretty tough. Bird Pokémon can peck at them all they want, and Cherrim won't be bothered at all.

Cherubi   Cherrim

Cherubi
Cherry Pokémon

How to Say It: chuh-ROO-bee
Imperial Height: 1'4"
Metric Height: 0.4 m
Imperial Weight: 7.3 lbs.
Metric Weight: 3.3 kg
Gender: ♂ ♀
Ability: Chorophyll
Weaknesses: Bug, Fire, Flying, Ice, Poison

POKÉMON SWORD:
It nimbly dashes about to avoid getting pecked by bird Pokémon that would love to make off with its small, nutrient-rich storage ball.

POKÉMON SHIELD:
The deeper a Cherubi's red, the more nutrients it has stockpiled in its body. And the sweeter and tastier its small ball!

Cherubi ⇨ Cherrim

Chewtle
Snapping Pokémon

How to Say It: CHOO-tull
Imperial Height: 1'
Metric Height: 0.3 m
Imperial Weight: 18.7 lbs.
Metric Weight: 8.5 kg
Gender: ♂ ♀
Ability: Strong Jaw / Shell Armor
Weaknesses: Grass, Electric

POKÉMON SWORD:
Apparently the itch of its teething impels it to snap its jaws at anything in front of it.

POKÉMON SHIELD:
It starts off battles by attacking with its rock-hard horn, but as soon as the opponent flinches, this Pokémon bites down and never lets go.

 ⇨

Chewtle ⇨ Drednaw

Chinchou

Angler Pokémon

How to Say It: CHIN-chow
Imperial Height: 1'8"
Metric Height: 0.5 m
Imperial Weight: 26.5 lbs.
Metric Weight: 12.0 kg
Gender: ♂ ♀
Ability: Volt Absorb / Illuminate
Weaknesses: Grass, Ground

POKÉMON SWORD:
Its antennae, which evolved from a fin, have both positive and negative charges flowing through them.

POKÉMON SHIELD:
On the dark ocean floor, its only means of communication is its constantly flashing lights.

Chinchou   Lanturn

Cinccino

Scarf Pokémon

How to Say It: chin-CHEE-noh
Imperial Height: 1'8"
Metric Height: 0.5 m
Imperial Weight: 16.5 lbs.
Metric Weight: 7.5 kg
Gender: ♂ ♀
Ability: Cute Charm / Technician
Weaknesses: Fighting

POKÉMON SWORD:
Its body secretes oil that this Pokémon spreads over its nest as a coating to protect it from dust. Cinccino won't tolerate even a speck of the stuff.

POKÉMON SHIELD:
A special oil that seeps through their fur helps them avoid attacks. The oil fetches a high price at market.

Minccino   Cinccino

Cinderace
Striker Pokémon

How to Say It: SIN-deh-race
Imperial Height: 4'7"
Metric Height: 1.4 m
Imperial Weight: 72.8 lbs.
Metric Weight: 33.0 kg
Gender: ♂ ♀
Ability: Blaze
Weaknesses: Water, Ground, Rock

POKÉMON SWORD:
It juggles a pebble with its feet, turning it into a burning soccer ball. Its shots strike opponents hard and leave them scorched.

POKÉMON SHIELD:
It's skilled at both offense and defense, and it gets pumped up when cheered on. But if it starts showboating, it could put itself in a tough spot.

Scorbunny ⇨ Raboot ⇨ Cinderace

Claydol
Clay Doll Pokémon

How to Say It: CLAY-doll
Imperial Height: 4'11"
Metric Height: 1.5 m
Imperial Weight: 238.1 lbs.
Metric Weight: 108 kg
Gender: Unknown
Ability: Levitate
Weaknesses: Bug, Dark, Ghost, Grass, Water, Ice

POKÉMON SWORD:
This mysterious Pokémon started life as an ancient clay figurine made over 20,000 years ago.

POKÉMON SHIELD:
It appears to have been born from clay dolls made by ancient people. It uses telekinesis to float and move.

Baltoy **Claydol**

Clefable
Fairy Pokémon

How to Say It: kleh-FAY-bull
Imperial Height: 4'3"
Metric Height: 1.3 m
Imperial Weight: 88.2 lbs.
Metric Weight: 40.0 kg
Gender: ♂ ♀
Ability: Cute Charm / Magic Guard
Weaknesses: Steel, Poison

POKÉMON SWORD:
A timid fairy Pokémon that is rarely seen, it will run and hide the moment it senses people.

POKÉMON SHIELD:
Their ears are sensitive enough to hear a pin drop from over a mile away, so they're usually found in quiet places.

Cleffa **Clefairy** **Clefable**

Clefairy
Fairy Pokémon

TYPE: Fairy

How to Say It: kleh-FAIR-ee
Imperial Height: 2'
Metric Height: 0.6 m
Imperial Weight: 16.5 lbs.
Metric Weight: 7.5 kg
Gender: ♂ ♀
Ability: Cute Charm / Magic Guard
Weaknesses: Steel, Poison

POKÉMON SWORD:
It is said that happiness will come to those who see a gathering of Clefairy dancing under a full moon.

POKÉMON SHIELD:
Its adorable behavior and cry make it highly popular. However, this cute Pokémon is rarely found.

Cleffa   Clefairy   Clefable

Cleffa
Star Shape Pokémon

TYPE: Fairy

How to Say It: CLEFF-uh
Imperial Height: 1'
Metric Height: 0.3 m
Imperial Weight: 6.6 lbs.
Metric Weight: 3.0 kg
Gender: ♂ ♀
Ability: Cute Charm / Magic Guard
Weaknesses: Steel, Poison

POKÉMON SWORD:
According to local rumors, Cleffa are often seen in places where shooting stars have fallen.

POKÉMON SHIELD:
Because of its unusual, starlike silhouette, people believe that it came here on a meteor.

Cleffa   Clefairy   Clefable

Clobbopus
Tantrum Pokémon

How to Say It: KLAH-buh-puss
Imperial Height: 2'
Metric Height: 0.6 m
Imperial Weight: 8.8 lbs.
Metric Weight: 4.0 kg
Gender: ♂ ♀
Ability: Limber
Weaknesses: Psychic, Flying, Fairy

POKÉMON SWORD:
It's very curious, but its means of investigating things is to try to punch them with its tentacles. The search for food is what brings it onto land.

POKÉMON SHIELD:
Its tentacles tear off easily, but it isn't alarmed when that happens—it knows they'll grow back. It's about as smart as a three-year-old.

Clobbopus → Grapploct

Cloyster
Bivalve Pokémon

TYPE:
Water-
Ice

How to Say It: CLOY-stur
Imperial Height: 4'11"
Metric Height: 1.5 m
Imperial Weight: 292 lbs.
Metric Weight: 132.5 kg
Gender: ♂ ♀
Ability: Shell Armor / Skill Link
Weaknesses: Electric, Fighting, Grass, Rock

POKÉMON SWORD:
Its shell is extremely hard. It cannot be shattered, even with a bomb. The shell opens only when it is attacking.

POKÉMON SHIELD:
Once it slams its shell shut, it is impossible to open, even by those with superior strength.

Shellder → Cloyster

Coalossal
Coal Pokémon

How to Say It: koh-LAHS-ull
Imperial Height: 9'2"
Metric Height: 2.8 m
Imperial Weight: 684.5 lbs.
Metric Weight: 310.5 kg
Gender: ♂ ♀
Ability: Steam Engine / Flame Body
Weaknesses: Water, Ground, Fighting, Rock

POKÉMON SWORD:
It's usually peaceful, but the vandalism of mines enrages it. Offenders will be incinerated with flames that reach 2,700 degrees Fahrenheit.

POKÉMON SHIELD:
While it's engaged in battle, its mountain of coal will burn bright red, sending off sparks that scorch the surrounding area.

Rolycoly   **Carkol**   **Coalossal**

Gigantamax Coalossal

Imperial Height: 137'10"+
Metric Height: 42.0+m
Imperial Weight: ?????.? lbs.
Metric Weight: ?????.? kg

POKÉMON SWORD:
Its body is a colossal stove. With Gigantamax energy stoking the fire, this Pokémon's flame burns hotter than 3,600 degrees Fahrenheit.

POKÉMON SHIELD:
When Galar was hit by a harsh cold wave, this Pokémon served as a giant heating stove and saved many lives.

Cofagrigus
Coffin Pokémon

TYPE:
Ghost

How to Say It: kof-uh-GREE-gus
Imperial Height: 5'7"
Metric Height: 1.7 m
Imperial Weight: 168.7 lbs.
Metric Weight: 76.5 kg
Gender: ♂ ♀
Ability: Mummy
Weaknesses: Ghost, Dark

POKÉMON SWORD:
This Pokémon has a body of sparkling gold. People say it no longer remembers that it was once human.

POKÉMON SHIELD:
There are many depictions of Cofagrigus decorating ancient tombs. They're symbols of the wealth that kings of bygone eras had.

Yamask ⇨ Cofagrigus

TYPE:
Bug-Flying

Combee
Tiny Bee Pokémon

How to Say It: COMB-bee
Imperial Height: 1'
Metric Height: 0.3 m
Imperial Weight: 12.1 lbs.
Metric Weight: 5.5 kg
Gender: ♂ ♀
Ability: Honey Gather
Weaknesses: Rock, Electric, Fire, Flying, Ice

POKÉMON SWORD:
The members of the trio spend all their time together. Each one has a slightly different taste in nectar.

POKÉMON SHIELD:
It ceaselessly gathers nectar from sunrise to sundown, all for the sake of Vespiquen and the swarm.

Combee ⇨ Vespiquen

Conkeldurr
Muscular Pokémon

How to Say It: kon-KELL-dur
Imperial Height: 4'7"
Metric Height: 1.4 m
Imperial Weight: 191.8 lbs.
Metric Weight: 87.0 kg
Gender: ♂ ♀
Ability: Guts / Sheer Force
Weaknesses: Flying, Psychic, Fairy

POKÉMON SWORD:
Concrete mixed by Conkeldurr is much more durable than normal concrete, even when the compositions of the two materials are the same.

POKÉMON SHIELD:
When going all out, this Pokémon throws aside its concrete pillars and leaps at opponents to pummel them with its fists.

Timburr ⇨ Gurdurr ⇨ Conkeldurr

Copperajah

Copperderm Pokémon

TYPE: Steel

How to Say It: KAH-peh-RAH-zhah
Imperial Height: 9'10"
Metric Height: 3.0 m
Imperial Weight: 1433.0 lbs.
Metric Weight: 650.0 kg
Gender: ♂ ♀
Ability: Sheer Force
Weaknesses: Fire, Fighting, Ground

POKÉMON SWORD:
They came over from another region long ago and worked together with humans. Their green skin is resistant to water.

POKÉMON SHIELD:
These Pokémon live in herds. Their trunks have incredible grip strength, strong enough to crush giant rocks into powder.

Cufant ⇨ Copperajah

Gigantamax Copperajah

Imperial Height: 75'6"+
Metric Height: 23.0+ m
Imperial Weight: ?????.? lbs.
Metric Weight: ?????.? kg

POKÉMON SWORD:
So much power is packed within its trunk that if it were to unleash that power, the resulting blast could level mountains and change the landscape.

POKÉMON SHIELD:
After this Pokémon has Gigantamaxed, its massive nose can utterly demolish large structures with a single smashing blow.

Corphish
Ruffian Pokémon

How to Say It: COR-fish
Imperial Height: 2'
Metric Height: 0.6 m
Imperial Weight: 25.4 lbs.
Metric Weight: 11.5 kg
Gender: ♂ ♀
Ability: Hyper Cutter / Shell Armor
Weaknesses: Electric, Grass

POKÉMON SWORD:
No matter how dirty the water in the river, it will adapt and thrive. It has a strong will to survive.

POKÉMON SHIELD:
It was originally a Pokémon from afar that escaped to the wild. It can adapt to the dirtiest river.

Corphish   Crawdaunt

GALARIAN
Corsola
Coral Pokémon

TYPE:
Ghost

How to Say It: COR-soh-la
Imperial Height: 2'
Metric Height: 0.6 m
Imperial Weight: 1.1 lbs.
Metric Weight: 0.5 kg
Gender: ♂ ♀
Ability: Weak Armor
Weaknesses: Ghost, Dark

POKÉMON SWORD:
Watch your step when wandering areas oceans once covered. What looks like a stone could be this Pokémon, and it will curse you if you kick it.

POKÉMON SHIELD:
Sudden climate change wiped out this ancient kind of Corsola. This Pokémon absorbs others' life-force through its branches.

Galarian Corsola   **Cursola**

Corviknight

Raven Pokémon

How to Say It: KOR-vih-nyte
Imperial Height: 7'3"
Metric Height: 2.2 m
Imperial Weight: 165.3 lbs.
Metric Weight: 75.0 kg
Gender: ♂ ♀
Ability: Pressure / Unnerve
Weaknesses: Fire, Electric

POKÉMON SWORD:
This Pokémon reigns supreme in the skies of the Galar region. The black luster of its steel body could drive terror into the heart of any foe.

POKÉMON SHIELD:
With their great intellect and flying skills, these Pokémon very successfully act as the Galar region's airborne taxi service.

Rookidee   Corvisquire   Corviknight

Gigantamax Corviknight

Imperial Height: 45'11"+
Metric Height: 14.0+ m
Imperial Weight: ?????.? lbs.
Metric Weight: ?????.? kg

POKÉMON SWORD:
Imbued with Gigantamax energy, its wings can whip up winds more forceful than any hurricane could muster. The gusts blow everything away.

POKÉMON SHIELD:
The eight feathers on its back are called blade birds, and they can launch off its body to attack foes independently.

Corvisquire

Raven Pokémon

TYPE: Flying

How to Say It: KOR-vih-skwyre
Imperial Height: 2'7"
Metric Height: 0.8 m
Imperial Weight: 35.3 lbs.
Metric Weight: 16.0 kg
Gender: ♂♀
Ability: Keen Eye / Unnerve
Weaknesses: Electric, Ice, Rock

POKÉMON SWORD:
Smart enough to use tools in battle, these Pokémon have been seen picking up rocks and flinging them or using ropes to wrap up enemies.

POKÉMON SHIELD:
The lessons of many harsh battles have taught it how to accurately judge an opponent's strength.

Rookidee   Corvisquire   Corviknight

Cottonee

Cotton Puff Pokémon

TYPE: Grass-Fairy

How to Say It: KAHT-ton-ee
Imperial Height: 1'
Metric Height: 0.3 m
Imperial Weight: 1.3 lbs.
Metric Weight: 0.6 kg
Gender: ♂♀
Ability: Prankster / Infiltrator
Weaknesses: Fire, Ice, Poison, Flying, Steel

POKÉMON SWORD:
It shoots cotton from its body to protect itself. If it gets caught up in hurricane-strength winds, it can get sent to the other side of the Earth.

POKÉMON SHIELD:
Weaving together the cotton of both Cottonee and Eldegoss produces exquisite cloth that's highly prized by many luxury brands.

Cottonee   Whimsicott

Cramorant

Gulp Pokémon

How to Say It: KRAM-uh-rent
Imperial Height: 2'7"
Metric Height: 0.8 m
Imperial Weight: 39.7 lbs.
Metric Weight: 18.0 kg
Gender: ♂ ♀
Ability: Gulp Missile
Weaknesses: Electric, Rock

POKÉMON SWORD:
It's so strong that it can knock out some opponents in a single hit, but it also may forget what it's battling midfight.

POKÉMON SHIELD:
This hungry Pokémon swallows Arrokuda whole. Occasionally, it makes a mistake and tries to swallow a Pokémon other than its preferred prey.

Does not evolve.

Crawdaun

Rogue Pokémon

How to Say It: CRAW-daunt
Imperial Height: 3'7"
Metric Height: 1.1 m
Imperial Weight: 72.3 lbs.
Metric Weight: 32.8 kg
Gender: ♂ ♀
Ability: Hyper Cutter / Shell Armor
Weaknesses: Bug, Electric, Fighting, Grass, Fairy

POKÉMON SWORD:
A rough customer that wildly flails its giant claws. It is said to be extremely hard to raise.

POKÉMON SHIELD:
A brutish Pokémon that loves to battle. It will crash itself into any foe that approaches its nest.

Corphish   Crawdaunt

Croagunk
Toxic Mouth Pokémon

How to Say It: CROW-gunk
Imperial Height: 2'4"
Metric Height: 0.7 m
Imperial Weight: 50.7 lbs.
Metric Weight: 23.0 kg
Gender: ♂ ♀
Ability: Anticipation / Dry Skin
Weaknesses: Psychic, Flying, Ground

POKÉMON SWORD:
It makes frightening noises with its poison-filled cheek sacs. When opponents flinch, Croagunk hits them with a poison jab.

POKÉMON SHIELD:
Once diluted, its poison becomes medicinal. This Pokémon came into popularity after a pharmaceutical company chose it as a mascot.

Croagunk   Toxicroak

TYPE:
Bug-Rock

Crustle
Stone Home Pokémon

How to Say It: KRUS-tul
Imperial Height: 4'7"
Metric Height: 1.4 m
Imperial Weight: 440.9 lbs.
Metric Weight: 200.0 kg
Gender: ♂ ♀
Ability: Sturdy / Shell Armor
Weaknesses: Water, Rock, Steel

POKÉMON SWORD:
This highly territorial Pokémon prefers dry climates. It won't come out of its boulder on rainy days.

POKÉMON SHIELD:
Its thick claws are its greatest weapons. They're mighty enough to crack Rhyperior's carapace.

Dwebble   Crustle

Cubchoo

Chill Pokémon

How to Say It: cub-CHOO
Imperial Height: 1'8"
Metric Height: 0.5 m
Imperial Weight: 18.7 lbs.
Metric Weight: 8.5 kg
Gender: ♂ ♀
Ability: Snow Cloak / Slush Rush
Weaknesses: Fire, Fighting, Rock, Steel

POKÉMON SWORD:
When this Pokémon is in good health, its snot becomes thicker and stickier. It will smear its snot on anyone it doesn't like.

POKÉMON SHIELD:
It sniffles before performing a move, using its frosty snot to provide an icy element to any move that needs it.

Cubchoo   Beartic

TYPE:
Steel

Cufant

Copperderm Pokémon

How to Say It: KYOO-funt
Imperial Height: 3'11"
Metric Height: 1.2 m
Imperial Weight: 220.5 lbs.
Metric Weight: 100.0 kg
Gender: ♂ ♀
Ability: Sheer Force
Weaknesses: Fire, Fighting, Ground

POKÉMON SWORD:
It digs up the ground with its trunk. It's also very strong, being able to carry loads of over five tons without any problem at all.

POKÉMON SHIELD:
If a job requires serious strength, this Pokémon will excel at it. Its copper body tarnishes in the rain, turning a vibrant green color.

Cufant   Copperajah

Cursola
Coral Pokémon

TYPE:
Ghost

How to Say It: KURR-suh-luh
Imperial Height: 3'3"
Metric Height: 1.0 m
Imperial Weight: 0.9 lbs.
Metric Weight: 0.4 kg
Gender: ♂♀
Ability: Weak Armor
Weaknesses: Ghost, Dark

POKÉMON SWORD:
Its shell is overflowing with its heightened otherworldly energy. The ectoplasm serves as protection for this Pokémon's core spirit.

POKÉMON SHIELD:
Be cautious of the ectoplasmic body surrounding its soul. You'll become stiff as stone if you touch it.

Galarian Corsola ⇨ Cursola

TYPE:
Bug-
Fairy

Cutiefly
Bee Fly Pokémon

How to Say It: KYOO-tee-FLY
Imperial Height: 4"
Metric Height: 0.1 m
Imperial Weight: 0.4 lbs.
Metric Weight: 0.2 kg
Gender: ♂♀
Ability: Honey Gather / Shield Dust
Weaknesses: Fire, Steel, Flying, Poison, Rock

POKÉMON SWORD:
Nectar and pollen are its favorite fare. You can find Cutiefly hovering around Gossifleur, trying to get some of Gossifleur's pollen.

POKÉMON SHIELD:
An opponent's aura can tell Cutiefly what that opponent's next move will be. Then Cutiefly can glide around the attack and strike back.

Cutiefly ⇨ Ribombee

GALARIAN
Darmanitan
Zen Charm Pokémon

TYPE:
Ice

How to Say It: dar-MAN-ih-tan
Imperial Height: 5'7"
Metric Height: 1.7 m
Imperial Weight: 264.6 lbs.
Metric Weight: 120.0 kg
Gender: ♂♀
Ability: Gorilla Tactics
Weaknesses: Fire, Steel, Fighting, Rock

POKÉMON SWORD:
On days when blizzards blow through, it comes down to where people live. It stashes food in the snowball on its head, taking it home for later.

POKÉMON SHIELD:
Though it has a gentle disposition, it's also very strong. It will quickly freeze the snowball on its head before going for a headbutt.

Galarian
Darumaka

Galarian
Darmanitan

GALARIAN
Darumaka
Zen Charm Pokémon

TYPE:
Ice

How to Say It: dah-roo-MAH-kuh
Imperial Height: 2'4"
Metric Height: 0.7 m
Imperial Weight: 88.2 lbs.
Metric Weight: 40.0 kg
Gender: ♂♀
Ability: Hustle
Weaknesses: Fire, Steel, Fighting, Rock

POKÉMON SWORD:
It lived in snowy areas for so long that its fire sac cooled off and atrophied. It now has an organ that generates cold instead.

POKÉMON SHIELD:
The colder they get, the more energetic they are. They freeze their breath to make snowballs, using them as ammo for playful snowball fights.

Galarian
Darumaka

Galarian
Darmanitan

Deino
Irate Pokémon

TYPE:
Dark-Dragon

How to Say It: DY-noh
Imperial Height: 2'7"
Metric Height: 0.8 m
Imperial Weight: 38.1 lbs.
Metric Weight: 17.3 kg
Gender: ♂ ♀
Ability: Hustle
Weaknesses: Ice, Fighting, Bug, Dragon, Fairy

POKÉMON SWORD:
When it encounters something, its first urge is usually to bite it. If it likes what it tastes, it will commit the associated scent to memory.

POKÉMON SHIELD:
Because it can't see, this Pokémon is constantly biting at everything it touches, trying to keep track of its surroundings.

Deino　Zweilous　Hydreigon

TYPE:
Ice-Flying

Delibird
Delivery Pokémon

How to Say It: DELL-ee-bird
Imperial Height: 2'11"
Metric Height: 0.9 m
Imperial Weight: 35.3
Metric Weight: 16.0 kg
Gender: ♂ ♀
Ability: Vital Spirit / Hustle
Weaknesses: Rock, Electric, Fire, Steel

POKÉMON SWORD:
It carries food all day long. There are tales about lost people who were saved by the food it had.

POKÉMON SHIELD:
It has a generous habit of sharing its food with people and Pokémon, so it's always scrounging around for more food.

Does not evolve.

Dewpider
Water Bubble Pokémon

TYPE:
Water-
Bug

How to Say It: DOO-pih-der
Imperial Height: 1'
Metric Height: 0.3 m
Imperial Weight: 8.8 lbs.
Metric Weight: 4.0 kg
Gender: ♂♀
Ability: Water Bubble
Weaknesses: Flying, Electric, Rock

POKÉMON SWORD:
It forms a water bubble at the rear of its body and then covers its head with it. Meeting another Dewpider means comparing water-bubble sizes.

POKÉMON SHIELD:
Dewpider normally lives underwater. When it comes onto land in search of food, it takes water with it in the form of a bubble on its head.

Dewpider   Araquanid

Dhelmise
Sea Creeper Pokémon

TYPE:
Ghost-
Grass

How to Say It: dell-MIZE
Imperial Height: 12'10"
Metric Height: 3.9 m
Imperial Weight: 463.0 lbs.
Metric Weight: 210.0 kg
Gender: Unknown
Ability: Steelworker
Weaknesses: Ghost, Fire, Flying, Dark, Ice

POKÉMON SWORD:
After a piece of seaweed merged with debris from a sunken ship, it was reborn as this ghost Pokémon.

POKÉMON SHIELD:
After lowering its anchor, it waits for its prey. It catches large Wailord and drains their life-force.

Does not evolve.

Diggersby
Digging Pokémon

TYPE:
Normal-Ground

How to Say It: DIH-gurz-bee
Imperial Height: 3'3"
Metric Height: 1.0 m
Imperial Weight: 93.5 lbs.
Metric Weight: 42.4 kg
Gender: ♂ ♀
Ability: Pickup / Cheek Pouch
Weaknesses: Water, Grass, Ice, Fighting

POKÉMON SWORD:
With power equal to an excavator, it can dig through dense bedrock. It's a huge help during tunnel construction.

POKÉMON SHIELD:
The fur on its belly retains heat exceptionally well. People used to make heavy winter clothing from fur shed by this Pokémon.

Bunnelby **Diggersby**

TYPE:
Ground

Diglett
Mole Pokémon

How to Say It: DIG-let
Imperial Height: 8"
Metric Height: 0.2 m
Imperial Weight: 1.8 lbs.
Metric Weight: 0.8 kg
Gender: ♂ ♀
Ability: Sand Veil / Arena Trap
Weaknesses: Grass, Ice, Water

POKÉMON SWORD:
If a Diglett digs through a field, it leaves the soil perfectly tilled and ideal for planting crops.

POKÉMON SHIELD:
It burrows through the ground at a shallow depth. It leaves raised earth in its wake, making it easy to spot.

Diglett **Dugtrio**

Ditto

Transform Pokémon

TYPE:
Normal

How to Say It: DIT-toe
Imperial Height: 1'
Metric Height: 0.3 m
Imperial Weight: 8.8 lbs.
Metric Weight: 4.0 kg
Gender: Unknown
Ability: Limber
Weaknesses: Fighting

POKÉMON SWORD:
It can reconstitute its entire cellular structure to change into what it sees, but it returns to normal when it relaxes.

POKÉMON SHIELD:
When it encounters another Ditto, it will move faster than normal to duplicate that opponent exactly.

Does not evolve.

TYPE:
Bug-Psychic

Dottler

Radome Pokémon

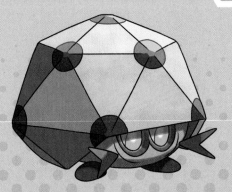

How to Say It: DOT-ler
Imperial Height: 1'4"
Metric Height: 0.4 m
Imperial Weight: 43.0 lbs.
Metric Weight: 19.5 kg
Gender: ♂ ♀
Ability: Swarm / Compound Eyes
Weaknesses: Ghost, Fire, Flying, Dark, Rock, Bug

POKÉMON SWORD:
It barely moves, but it's still alive. Hiding in its shell without food or water seems to have awakened its psychic powers.

POKÉMON SHIELD:
As it grows inside its shell, it uses its psychic abilities to monitor the outside world and prepare for evolution.

Blipbug **Dottler** **Orbeetle**

Doublade
Sword Pokémon

How to Say It: DUH-blade
Imperial Height: 2'7"
Metric Height: 0.8 m
Imperial Weight: 9.9 lbs.
Metric Weight: 4.5 kg
Gender: ♂ ♀
Ability: No Guard
Weaknesses: Fire, Ghost, Dark, Ground

POKÉMON SWORD:
Honedge evolves into twins. The two blades rub together to emit a metallic sound that unnerves opponents.

POKÉMON SHIELD:
The two swords employ a strategy of rapidly alternating between offense and defense to bring down their prey.

 ⇨ ⇨

Honedge   **Doublade**   **Aegislash**

TYPE:
Water-Dragon

Dracovish
Fossil Pokémon

How to Say It: DRAK-oh-vish
Imperial Height: 7'7"
Metric Height: 2.3 m
Imperial Weight: 474.0 lbs.
Metric Weight: 215.0 kg
Gender: Unknown
Ability: Water Absorb / Strong Jaw
Weaknesses: Fairy, Dragon

POKÉMON SWORD:
Powerful legs and jaws made it the apex predator of its time. Its own overhunting of its prey was what drove it to extinction.

POKÉMON SHIELD:
Its mighty legs are capable of running at speeds exceeding 40 mph, but this Pokémon can't breathe unless it's underwater.

Does not evolve.

Dracozolt

Fossil Pokémon

How to Say It: DRAK-oh-zohlt
Imperial Height: 5'11"
Metric Height: 1.8 m
Imperial Weight: 418.9 lbs.
Metric Weight: 190.0 kg
Gender: Unknown
Ability: Volt Absorb / Hustle
Weaknesses: Fairy, Ground, Ice, Dragon

POKÉMON SWORD:
In ancient times, it was unbeatable thanks to its powerful lower body, but it went extinct anyway after it depleted all its plant-based food sources.

POKÉMON SHIELD:
The powerful muscles in its tail generate its electricity. Compared to its lower body, its upper half is entirely too small.

Does not evolve.

Dragapult
Stealth Pokémon

How to Say It: DRAG-uh-pult
Imperial Height: 9'10"
Metric Height: 3.0 m
Imperial Weight: 110.2 lbs.
Metric Weight: 50.0 kg
Gender: ♂ ♀
Ability: Clear Body / Infiltrator
Weaknesses: Ghost, Dark, Fairy,
Ice, Dragon

POKÉMON SWORD:
When it isn't battling, it keeps Dreepy in the holes on its horns. Once a fight starts, it launches the Dreepy-like supersonic missiles.

POKÉMON SHIELD:
Apparently the Dreepy inside Dragapult's horns eagerly look forward to being launched out at Mach speeds.

Dreepy   Drakloak   Dragapult

Drakloak
Caretaker Pokémon

How to Say It: DRAK-klohk
Imperial Height: 4'7"
Metric Height: 1.4 m
Imperial Weight: 24.3 lbs.
Metric Weight: 11.0 kg
Gender: ♂ ♀
Ability: Clear Body / Infiltrator
Weaknesses: Ghost, Dark, Fairy, Ice, Dragon

POKÉMON SWORD:
It's capable of flying faster than 120 mph. It battles alongside Dreepy and dotes on them until they successfully evolve.

POKÉMON SHIELD:
Without a Dreepy to place on its head and care for, it gets so uneasy it'll try to substitute any Pokémon it finds for the missing Dreepy.

Dreepy   Drakloak   Dragapult

Drampa

Placid Pokémon

TYPE:
Normal-
Dragon

How to Say It: DRAM-puh
Imperial Height: 9'10"
Metric Height: 3.0 m
Imperial Weight: 407.9 lbs.
Metric Weight: 185.0 kg
Gender: ♂♀
Ability: Berserk / Sap Sipper
Weaknesses: Fairy, Fighting, Ice, Dragon

POKÉMON SWORD:
The mountains it calls home are nearly two miles in height. On rare occasions, it descends to play with the children living in the towns below.

POKÉMON SHIELD:
Drampa is a kind and friendly Pokémon—up until it's angered. When that happens, it stirs up a gale and flattens everything around.

Does not evolve.

Drapion

Ogre Scorpion Pokémo

TYPE:
Poison-
Dark

How to Say It: DRAP-ee-on
Imperial Height: 4'3"
Metric Height: 1.3 m
Imperial Weight: 135.6 lbs.
Metric Weight: 61.5 kg
Gender: ♂♀
Ability: Battle Armor / Sniper
Weaknesses: Ground

POKÉMON SWORD:
Its poison is potent, but it rarely sees use. This Pokémon prefers to use physical force instead, going on rampages with its car-crushing strength.

POKÉMON SHIELD:
It's so vicious that it's called the Sand Demon. Yet when confronted by Hippowdon, Drapion keeps a low profile and will never pick a fight.

Skorupi ⇨ Drapion

Drednaw
Bite Pokémon

TYPE: Water-Rock

How to Say It: DRED-naw
Imperial Height: 3'3"
Metric Height: 1.0 m
Imperial Weight: 254.6 lbs.
Metric Weight: 115.5 kg
Gender: ♂♀
Ability: Strong Jaw / Shell Armor
Weaknesses: Grass, Electric, Fighting, Ground

POKÉMON SWORD:
With jaws that can shear through steel rods, this highly aggressive Pokémon chomps down on its unfortunate prey.

POKÉMON SHIELD:
This Pokémon rapidly extends its retractable neck to sink its sharp fangs into distant enemies and take them down.

Chewtle ➡ **Drednaw**

Gigantamax Drednaw

Imperial Height: 78'9"+
Metric Height: 24.0+ m
Imperial Weight: ????.? lbs.
Metric Weight: ????.? kg

POKÉMON SWORD:
It responded to Gigantamax energy by becoming bipedal. First it comes crashing down on foes, and then it finishes them off with its massive jaws.

POKÉMON SHIELD:
In the Galar region, there's a tale about this Pokémon chewing up a mountain and using the rubble to stop a flood.

Dreepy
Lingering Pokémon

How to Say It: DREE-pee
Imperial Height: 1'8"
Metric Height: 0.5 m
Imperial Weight: 4.4 lbs.
Metric Weight: 2.0 kg
Gender: ♂ ♀
Ability: Clear Body / Infiltrator
Weaknesses: Ghost, Dark, Fairy, Ice, Dragon

POKÉMON SWORD:
After being reborn as a ghost Pokémon, Dreepy wanders the areas it used to inhabit back when it was alive in prehistoric seas.

POKÉMON SHIELD:
If this weak Pokémon is by itself, a mere child could defeat it. But if Dreepy has friends to help it train, it can evolve and become much stronger.

Dreepy ➡ **Drakloak** ➡ **Dragapu**

Drifblim
Blimp Pokémon

TYPE: Ghost-Flying

How to Say It: DRIFF-blim
Imperial Height: 3'11"
Metric Height: 1.2 m
Imperial Weight: 33.1 lbs.
Metric Weight: 15.0 kg
Gender: ♂ ♀
Ability: Aftermath / Unburden
Weaknesses: Dark, Electric, Ghost, Ice, Rock

POKÉMON SWORD:
Some say this Pokémon is a collection of souls burdened with regrets, silently drifting through the dusk.

POKÉMON SHIELD:
It grabs people and Pokémon and carries them off somewhere. Where do they go? Nobody knows.

Drifloon ➡ **Drifblim**

Drifloon

Balloon Pokémon

TYPE:
Ghost-
Flying

How to Say It: DRIFF-loon
Imperial Height: 1'4"
Metric Height: 0.4 m
Imperial Weight: 2.6 lbs.
Metric Weight: 1.2 kg
Gender: ♂ ♀
Ability: Aftermath / Unburden
Weaknesses: Dark, Electric, Ghost, Ice, Rock

POKÉMON SWORD:
Perhaps seeking company, it approaches children. However, it often quickly runs away again when the children play too roughly with it.

POKÉMON SHIELD:
The gathering of many souls gave rise to this Pokémon. During humid seasons, they seem to appear in abundance.

Drifloon ➡ Drifblim

Drilbur

Mole Pokémon

TYPE:
Ground

How to Say It: DRIL-bur
Imperial Height: 1'
Metric Height: 0.3 m
Imperial Weight: 18.7 lbs.
Metric Weight: 8.5 kg
Gender: ♂ ♀
Ability: Sand Rush / Sand Force
Weaknesses: Water, Grass, Ice

POKÉMON SWORD:
It brings its claws together and whirls around at high speed before rushing toward its prey.

POKÉMON SHIELD:
It's a digger, using its claws to burrow through the ground. It causes damage to vegetable crops, so many farmers have little love for it.

 ➡

Drilbur ➡ Excadrill

Drizzile
Water Lizard Pokémon

How to Say It: DRIZ-zyle
Imperial Height: 2'4"
Metric Height: 0.7 m
Imperial Weight: 25.4 lbs.
Metric Weight: 11.5 kg
Gender: ♂♀
Ability: Torrent
Weaknesses: Grass, Electric

POKÉMON SWORD:
A clever combatant, this Pokémon battles using water balloons created with moisture secreted from its palms.

POKÉMON SHIELD:
Highly intelligent but also very lazy, it keeps enemies out of its territory by laying traps everywhere.

Sobble   Drizzile   Inteleon

Dubwool
Sheep Pokémon

How to Say It: DUB-wool
Imperial Height: 4'3"
Metric Height: 1.3 m
Imperial Weight: 94.8 lbs.
Metric Weight: 43.0 kg
Gender: ♂♀
Ability: Fluffy / Steadfast
Weaknesses: Fighting

POKÉMON SWORD:
Weave a carpet from its springy wool, and you end up with something closer to a trampoline. You'll start to bounce the moment you set foot on it.

POKÉMON SHIELD:
Its majestic horns are meant only to impress the opposite gender. They never see use in battle.

Wooloo   Dubwool

Dugtrio
Mole Pokémon

TYPE: Ground

How to Say It: DUG-TREE-oh
Imperial Height: 2'4"
Metric Height: 0.7 m
Imperial Weight: 73.4 lbs.
Metric Weight: 33.3 kg
Gender: ♂ ♀
Ability: Sand Veil / Arena Trap
Weaknesses: Grass, Ice, Water

POKÉMON SWORD:
A team of Diglett triplets. It triggers huge earthquakes by burrowing 60 miles underground.

POKÉMON SHIELD:
These Diglett triplets dig over 60 miles below sea level. No one knows what it's like that far underground.

Diglett **Dugtrio**

TYPE: Psychic

Duosion
Mitosis Pokémon

How to Say It: doo-OH-zhun
Imperial Height: 2'
Metric Height: 0.6 m
Imperial Weight: 17.6 lbs.
Metric Weight: 8.0 kg
Gender: ♂ ♀
Ability: Overcoat / Magic Guard
Weaknesses: Bug, Ghost, Dark

POKÉMON SWORD:
Its psychic power can supposedly cover a range of more than half a mile—but only if its two brains can agree with each other.

POKÉMON SHIELD:
Its brain has split into two, and the two halves rarely think alike. Its actions are utterly unpredictable.

Solosis **Duosion** **Reuniclus**

Duraludon

Alloy Pokémon

How to Say It: duh-RAL-uh-dahn
Imperial Height: 5'11"
Metric Height: 1.8 m
Imperial Weight: 88.2 lbs.
Metric Weight: 40.0 kg
Gender: ♂♀
Ability: Light Metal / Heavy Metal
Weaknesses: Fighting, Ground

POKÉMON SWORD:
Its body resembles polished metal, and it's both lightweight and strong. The only drawback is that it rusts easily.

POKÉMON SHIELD:
The special metal that composes its body is very light, so this Pokémon has considerable agility. It lives in caves because it dislikes the rain.

Does not evolve.

Gigantamax Duraludon

Imperial Height: 141'1"+
Metric Height: 43.0+ m
Imperial Weight: ????.? lbs.
Metric Weight: ????.? kg

POKÉMON SWORD:
It's grown to resemble a skyscraper. Parts of its towering body glow due to a profusion of energy.

POKÉMON SHIELD:
The hardness of its cells is exceptional, even among Steel types. It also has a body structure that's resistant to earthquakes.

Durant

Iron Ant Pokémon

TYPE:
Bug-Steel

How to Say It: dur-ANT
Imperial Height: 1'
Metric Height: 0.3 m
Imperial Weight: 72.8 lbs.
Metric Weight: 33.0 kg
Gender: ♂♀
Ability: Swarm / Hustle
Weaknesses: Fire

POKÉMON SWORD:
They lay their eggs deep inside their nests. When attacked by Heatmor, they retaliate using their massive mandibles.

POKÉMON SHIELD:
With their large mandibles, these Pokémon can crunch their way through rock. They work together to protect their eggs from Sandaconda.

Does not evolve.

Dusclops

Beckon Pokémon

TYPE:
Ghost

How to Say It: DUS-klops
Imperial Height: 5'3"
Metric Height: 1.6 m
Imperial Weight: 67.5 lbs.
Metric Weight: 30.6 kg
Gender: ♂♀
Ability: Pressure
Weaknesses: Dark, Ghost

POKÉMON SWORD:
Its body is entirely hollow. When it opens its mouth, it sucks everything in as if it were a black hole.

POKÉMON SHIELD:
It seeks drifting will-o'-the-wisps and sucks them into its empty body. What happens inside is a mystery.

Duskull ⇨ Dusclops ⇨ Dusknoir

usknoir

Gripper Pokémon

How to Say It: DUSK-nwar
Imperial Height: 7'3"
Metric Height: 2.2 m
Imperial Weight: 235.0 lbs.
Metric Weight: 106.6 kg
Gender: ♂ ♀
Ability: Pressure
Weaknesses: Dark, Ghost

POKÉMON SWORD:
At the bidding of transmissions from the spirit world, it steals people and Pokémon away. No one knows whether it has a will of its own.

POKÉMON SHIELD:
With the mouth on its belly, Dusknoir swallows its target whole. The soul is the only thing eaten—Dusknoir disgorges the body before departing.

Duskull   **Dusclops**   **Duskno**

**TYPE:
Ghost**

Duskull

Requiem Pokémon

How to Say It: DUS-kull
Imperial Height: 2'7"
Metric Height: 0.8 m
Imperial Weight: 33.1 lbs.
Metric Weight: 15.0 kg
Gender: ♂ ♀
Ability: Levitate
Weaknesses: Dark, Ghost

POKÉMON SWORD:
If it finds bad children who won't listen to their parents, it will spirit them away—or so it's said.

POKÉMON SHIELD:
Making itself invisible, it silently sneaks up on prey. It has the ability to slip through thick walls.

Duskull   **Dusclops**   **Dusknoir**

Dwebble
Rock Inn Pokémon

How to Say It: DWEHB-bul
Imperial Height: 1'
Metric Height: 0.3 m
Imperial Weight: 32.0 lbs.
Metric Weight: 14.5 kg
Gender: ♂ ♀
Ability: Sturdy / Shell Armor
Weaknesses: Water, Rock, Steel

POKÉMON SWORD:
When it finds a stone appealing, it creates a hole inside it and uses it as its home. This Pokémon is the natural enemy of Roggenrola and Rolycoly.

POKÉMON SHIELD:
It first tries to find a rock to live in, but if there are no suitable rocks to be found, Dwebble may move in to the ports of a Hippowdon.

Dwebble ⇨ Crustle

Eevee

Evolution Pokémon

How to Say It: EE-vee
Imperial Height: 1'
Metric Height: 0.3 m
Imperial Weight: 14.3 lbs.
Metric Weight: 6.5 kg
Gender: ♂ ♀
Ability: Run Away / Adaptability
Weaknesses: Fighting

POKÉMON SWORD:
It has the ability to alter the composition of its body to suit its surrounding environment.

POKÉMON SHIELD:
Thanks to its unstable genetic makeup, this special Pokémon conceals many different possible evolutions.

Jolteon

Flareon

Glaceon

Vaporeon

Espeon

Eevee

Umbreon

Sylveon

Leafeon

Gigantamax Eevee

Imperial Height: 59'1"+
Metric Height: 18+ m
Imperial Weight: ?????.? lbs.
Metric Weight: ?????.? kg

POKÉMON SWORD:
Gigantamax energy upped the fluffiness of the fur around Eevee's neck. The fur will envelop a foe, capturing its body and captivating its mind.

POKÉMON SHIELD:
Having gotten even friendlier and more innocent, Eevee tries to play with anyone around, only to end up crushing them with its immense body.

Eiscue

Penguin Pokémon

How to Say It: ICE-kyoo
Imperial Height: 4'7"
Metric Height: 1.4 m
Imperial Weight: 196.2 lbs.
Metric Weight: 89.0 kg
Gender: ♂ ♀
Ability: Ice Face
Weaknesses: Fire, Steel, Fighting, Rock

POKÉMON SWORD:
It drifted in on the flow of ocean waters from a frigid place. It keeps its head iced constantly to make sure it stays nice and cold.

POKÉMON SHIELD:
This Pokémon keeps its heat-sensitive head cool with ice. It fishes for its food, dangling its single hair into the sea to lure in prey.

Does not evolve.

Eldegoss
Cotton Bloom Pokémon

How to Say It: EL-duh-gahs
Imperial Height: 1'8"
Metric Height: 0.5 m
Imperial Weight: 5.5 lbs.
Metric Weight: 2.5 kg
Gender: ♂♀
Ability: Cotton Down / Regenerator
Weaknesses: Fire, Flying, Ice, Poison, Bug

POKÉMON SWORD:
The seeds attached to its cotton fluff are full of nutrients. It spreads them on the wind so that plants and other Pokémon can benefit from them.

POKÉMON SHIELD:
The cotton on the head of this Pokémon can be spun into a glossy, gorgeous yarn—a Galar regional specialty.

Gossifleur ➡ Eldegoss

Electrike
Lightning Pokémon

TYPE: Electric

How to Say It: eh-LEK-trike
Imperial Height: 2'
Metric Height: 0.6 m
Imperial Weight: 33.5 lbs.
Metric Weight: 15.2 kg
Gender: ♂♀
Ability: Static / Lightning Rod
Weaknesses: Ground

POKÉMON SWORD:
It stores static electricity in its fur for discharging. It gives off sparks if a storm approaches.

POKÉMON SHIELD:
It stores electricity in its fur. It gives off sparks from all over its body in seasons when the air is dry.

Electrike ➡ Manectric

Elgyem
Cerebral Pokémon

TYPE:
Psychic

How to Say It: ELL-jee-ehm
Imperial Height: 1'8"
Metric Height: 0.5 m
Imperial Weight: 19.8 lbs.
Metric Weight: 9.0 kg
Gender: ♂ ♀
Ability: Telepathy / Synchronize
Weaknesses: Bug, Ghost, Dark

POKÉMON SWORD:
If this Pokémon stands near a TV, strange scenery will appear on the screen. That scenery is said to be from its home.

POKÉMON SHIELD:
This Pokémon was discovered about 50 years ago. Its highly developed brain enables it to exert its psychic powers.

Elgyem **Beheeyem**

TYPE:
Bug-Steel

Escavalier
Cavalry Pokémon

How to Say It: ess-KAV-a-LEER
Imperial Height: 3'3"
Metric Height: 1.0 m
Imperial Weight: 72.8 lbs.
Metric Weight: 33.0 kg
Gender: ♂ ♀
Ability: Swarm / Shell Armor
Weaknesses: Fire

POKÉMON SWORD:
They use shells they've stolen from Shelmet to arm and protect themselves. They're very popular Pokémon in the Galar region.

POKÉMON SHIELD:
It charges its enemies, lances at the ready. An image of one of its duels is captured in a famous painting of Escavalier clashing with Sirfetch'd.

Karrablast **Escavalier**

Espeon
Sun Pokémon

How to Say It: ESS-pee-on
Imperial Height: 2'11"
Metric Height: 0.9 m
Imperial Weight: 58.4 lbs.
Metric Weight: 26.5 kg
Gender: ♂ ♀
Ability: Synchronize
Weaknesses: Bug, Dark, Ghost

POKÉMON SWORD:
By reading air currents, it can predict things such as the weather or its foe's next move.

POKÉMON SHIELD:
It unleashes psychic power from the orb on its forehead. When its power is exhausted, the orb grows dull and dark.

Eevee ⇨ Espeon

Espurr
Restraint Pokémon

How to Say It: ESS-purr
Imperial Height: 1'
Metric Height: 0.3 m
Imperial Weight: 7.7 lbs.
Metric Weight: 3.5 kg
Gender: ♂ ♀
Ability: Keen Eye / Infiltrator
Weaknesses: Ghost, Dark, Bug

POKÉMON SWORD:
Though Espurr's expression never changes, behind that blank stare is an intense struggle to contain its devastating psychic power.

POKÉMON SHIELD:
There's enough psychic power in Espurr to send a wrestler flying, but because this power can't be controlled, Espurr finds it troublesome.

Espurr ⇨ Meowstic (male)
⇨ Meowstic (female)

TYPE: Poison-Dragon

Eternatus
Gigantic Pokémon

How to Say It: ee-TURR-nuh-tuss
Imperial Height: 65'7"
Metric Height: 20.0 m
Imperial Weight: 2094.4 lbs.
Metric Weight: 950.0 kg
Gender: Unknown
Ability: Pressure
Weaknesses: Psychic, Ground, Ice, Dragon

POKÉMON SWORD:
The core on its chest absorbs energy emanating from the lands of the Galar region. This energy is what allows Eternatus to stay active.

POKÉMON SHIELD:
It was inside a meteorite that fell 20,000 years ago. There seems to be a connection between this Pokémon and the Dynamax phenomenon.

Does not evolve.

Excadrill

Subterrene Pokémon

TYPE: Ground-Steel

How to Say It: EKS-kuh-drill
Imperial Height: 2'4"
Metric Height: 0.7 m
Imperial Weight: 89.1 lbs.
Metric Weight: 40.4 kg
Gender: ♂ ♀
Ability: Sand Rush / Sand Force
Weaknesses: Fire, Water, Fighting, Ground

POKÉMON SWORD:
It's not uncommon for tunnels that appear to have formed naturally to actually be a result of Excadrill's rampant digging.

POKÉMON SHIELD:
Known as the Drill King, this Pokémon can tunnel through the terrain at speeds of over 90 mph.

Drilbur ⇨ Excadrill

TYPE: Fighting

Falinks

Formation Pokémon

How to Say It: FAY-links
Imperial Height: 9'10"
Metric Height: 3.0 m
Imperial Weight: 136.7 lbs.
Metric Weight: 62.0 kg
Gender: Unknown
Ability: Battle Armor
Weaknesses: Psychic, Flying, Fairy

POKÉMON SWORD:
Five of them are troopers, and one is the brass. The brass's orders are absolute.

POKÉMON SHIELD:
The six of them work together as one Pokémon. Teamwork is also their battle strategy, and they constantly change their formation as they fight.

Does not evolve.

GALARIAN
Farfetch'd
Wild Duck Pokémon

How to Say It: FAR-fetched
Imperial Height: 2'7"
Metric Height: 0.8 m
Imperial Weight: 92.6 lbs.
Metric Weight: 42.0 kg
Gender: ♂ ♀
Ability: Steadfast
Weaknesses: Psychic, Flying, Fairy

POKÉMON SWORD:
The Farfetch'd of the Galar region are brave warriors, and they wield thick, tough leeks in battle.

POKÉMON SHIELD:
The stalks of leeks are thicker and longer in the Galar region. Farfetch'd that adapted to these stalks took on a unique form.

Galarian
Farfetch'd ➡ Sirfetch'd

TYPE:
Water

Feebas
Fish Pokémon

How to Say It: FEE-bass
Imperial Height: 2'
Metric Height: 0.6 m
Imperial Weight: 16.3 lbs.
Metric Weight: 7.4 kg
Gender: ♂ ♀
Ability: Swift Swim / Oblivious
Weaknesses: Electric, Grass

POKÉMON SWORD:
Although unattractive and unpopular, this Pokémon's marvelous vitality has made it a subject of research.

POKÉMON SHIELD:
It is a shabby and ugly Pokémon. However, it is very hardy and can survive on little water.

Feebas ➡ Milotic

Ferroseed

Thorn Seed Pokémon

How to Say It: fer-AH-seed
Imperial Height: 2'
Metric Height: 0.6 m
Imperial Weight: 41.4 lbs.
Metric Weight: 18.8 kg
Gender: ♂ ♀
Ability: Iron Barbs
Weaknesses: Fire, Fighting

POKÉMON SWORD:
It defends itself by launching spikes, but its aim isn't very good at first. Only after a lot of practice will it improve.

POKÉMON SHIELD:
Mossy caves are their preferred dwellings. Enzymes contained in mosses help Ferroseed's spikes grow big and strong.

Ferroseed   Ferrothorn

Ferrothorn

Thorn Pod Pokémon

TYPE:
Grass-
Steel

How to Say It: fer-AH-thorn
Imperial Height: 3'3"
Metric Height: 1.0 m
Imperial Weight: 242.5 lbs.
Metric Weight: 110.0 kg
Gender: ♂ ♀
Ability: Iron Barbs
Weaknesses: Fire, Fighting

POKÉMON SWORD:
This Pokémon scrapes its spikes across rocks, and then uses the tips of its feelers to absorb the nutrients it finds within the stone.

POKÉMON SHIELD:
Its spikes are harder than steel. This Pokémon crawls across rock walls by stabbing the spikes on its feelers into the stone.

Ferroseed   Ferrothorn

Flapple
Apple Wing Pokémon

How to Say It: FLAP-puhl
Imperial Height: 1'
Metric Height: 0.3 m
Imperial Weight: 2.2 lbs.
Metric Weight: 1.0 kg
Gender: ♂ ♀
Ability: Ripen / Gluttony
Weaknesses: Flying, Ice, Dragon, Poison, Fairy, Bug

POKÉMON SWORD:
It ate a sour apple, and that induced its evolution. In its cheeks, it stores an acid capable of causing chemical burns.

POKÉMON SHIELD:
It flies on wings of apple skin and spits a powerful acid. It can also change its shape into that of an apple.

Appletun

Applin

Flapple

Gigantamax Flapple

Imperial Height: 78'9"+
Metric Height: 24.0+ m
Imperial Weight: ?????.? lbs.
Metric Weight: ?????.? kg

POKÉMON SWORD:
Under the influence of Gigantamax energy, it produces much more sweet nectar, and its shape has changed to resemble a giant apple.

POKÉMON SHIELD:
If it stretches its neck, the strong aroma of its nectar pours out. The scent is so sickeningly sweet that one whiff makes other Pokémon faint.

Flareon

Flame Pokémon

TYPE:
Fire

How to Say It: FLAIR-ee-on
Imperial Height: 2'11"
Metric Height: 0.9 m
Imperial Weight: 55.1 lbs.
Metric Weight: 25.0 kg
Gender: ♂ ♀
Ability: Flash Fire
Weaknesses: Ground, Rock, Water

POKÉMON SWORD:
Once it has stored up enough heat, this Pokémon's body temperature can reach up to 1,700 degrees Fahrenheit.

POKÉMON SHIELD:
It stores some of the air it inhales in its internal flame pouch, which heats it to over 3,000 degrees Fahrenheit.

Eevee ⇨ Flareon

Flygon

Mystic Pokémon

TYPE:
Ground-
Dragon

How to Say It: FLY-gon
Imperial Height: 6'7"
Metric Height: 2.0 m
Imperial Weight: 180.8 lbs.
Metric Weight: 82.0 kg
Gender: ♂ ♀
Ability: Levitate
Weaknesses: Ice, Dragon, Fairy

POKÉMON SWORD:
This Pokémon hides in the heart of sandstorms it creates and seldom appears where people can see it.

POKÉMON SHIELD:
It is nicknamed the Desert Spirit because the flapping of its wings sounds like a woman singing.

Trapinch ⇨ Vibrava ⇨ Flygon

Fraxure

Axe Jaw Pokémon

How to Say It: FRAK-shur
Imperial Height: 3'3"
Metric Height: 1.0 m
Imperial Weight: 79.4 lbs.
Metric Weight: 36.0 kg
Gender: ♂♀
Ability: Rivalry / Mold Breaker
Weaknesses: Ice, Dragon, Fairy

POKÉMON SWORD:
After battle, this Pokémon carefully sharpens its tusks on river rocks. It needs to take care of its tusks—if one breaks, it will never grow back.

POKÉMON SHIELD:
Its skin is as hard as a suit of armor. Fraxure's favorite strategy is to tackle its opponents, stabbing them with its tusks at the same time.

Axew　　Fraxure　　Haxorus

TYPE:
Water-Ghost

Frillish

Floating Pokémon

Male Form

Female Form

How to Say It: FRIL-lish
Imperial Height: 3'11"
Metric Height: 1.2 m
Imperial Weight: 72.8 lbs.
Metric Weight: 33.0 kg
Gender: ♂♀
Ability: Water Absorb / Cursed Body
Weaknesses: Grass, Electric, Ghost, Dark

POKÉMON SWORD:
It envelops its prey in its veillike arms and draws it down to the deeps, five miles below the ocean's surface.

POKÉMON SHIELD:
Legend has it that the residents of a sunken ancient city changed into these Pokémon.

Frillish　　Jellicent

Froslass

Snow Land Pokémon

How to Say It: FROS-lass
Imperial Height: 4'3"
Metric Height: 1.3 m
Imperial Weight: 58.6 lbs.
Metric Weight: 26.6 kg
Gender: ♀
Ability: Snow Cloak
Weaknesses: Dark, Fire, Ghost, Rock, Steel

POKÉMON SWORD:
After a woman met her end on a snowy mountain, her regrets lingered on. From them, this Pokémon was born. Its favorite food is frozen souls.

POKÉMON SHIELD:
It spits out cold air of nearly −60 degrees Fahrenheit to freeze its quarry. It brings frozen prey back to its lair and neatly lines them up.

Snorunt

Froslass

Glalie

Frosmoth

Frost Moth Pokémon

How to Say It: FRAHS-mahth
Imperial Height: 4'3"
Metric Height: 1.3 m
Imperial Weight: 92.6 lbs.
Metric Weight: 42.0 kg
Gender: ♂ ♀
Ability: Shield Dust
Weaknesses: Fire, Steel, Flying, Rock

POKÉMON SWORD:
Icy scales fall from its wings like snow as it flies over fields and mountains. The temperature of its wings is less than −290 degrees Fahrenheit.

POKÉMON SHIELD:
It shows no mercy to any who desecrate fields and mountains. It will fly around on its icy wings, causing a blizzard to chase offenders away.

Snom

Frosmoth

Gallade
Blade Pokémon

TYPE: Psychic-Fighting

How to Say It: guh-LADE
Imperial Height: 5'3"
Metric Height: 1.6 m
Imperial Weight: 114.6 lbs.
Metric Weight: 52.0 kg
Gender: ♂
Ability: Steadfast
Weaknesses: Flying, Ghost, Fairy

POKÉMON SWORD:
True to its honorable-warrior image, it uses the blades on its elbows only in defense of something or someone.

POKÉMON SHIELD:
Sharply attuned to others' wishes for help, this Pokémon seeks out those in need and aids them in battle.

Gardevoir

Ralts ➡ Kirlia ➡ Gallade

TYPE: Bug-Electric

Galvantula
EleSpider Pokémon

How to Say It: gal-VAN-choo-luh
Imperial Height: 2'7"
Metric Height: 0.8 m
Imperial Weight: 31.5 lbs.
Metric Weight: 14.3 kg
Gender: ♂ ♀
Ability: Compound Eyes / Unnerve
Weaknesses: Fire, Rock

POKÉMON SWORD:
It launches electrified fur from its abdomen as its means of attack. Opponents hit by the fur could be in for three full days and nights of paralysis.

POKÉMON SHIELD:
It lays traps of electrified threads near the nests of bird Pokémon, aiming to snare chicks that are not yet good at flying.

 ➡

Joltik   Galvantula

Garbodor

Trash Heap Pokémon

How to Say It: gar-BOH-dur
Imperial Height: 6'3"
Metric Height: 1.9 m
Imperial Weight: 236.6 lbs.
Metric Weight: 107.3 kg
Gender: ♂ ♀
Ability: Stench / Weak Armor
Weaknesses: Ground, Psychic

POKÉMON SWORD:
This Pokémon eats trash, which turns into poison inside its body. The main component of the poison depends on what sort of trash was eaten.

POKÉMON SHIELD:
The toxic liquid it launches from its right arm is so virulent that it can kill a weakened creature instantly.

Trubbish ⇒ Garbodor

Gigantamax Garbodor

Imperial Height: 68'11"+
Metric Height: 21.0+ m
Imperial Weight: ?????.? lbs.
Metric Weight: ?????.? kg

POKÉMON SWORD:
Due to Gigantamax energy, this Pokémon's toxic gas has become much thicker, congealing into masses shaped like discarded toys.

POKÉMON SHIELD:
It sprays toxic gas from its mouth and fingers. If the gas engulfs you, the toxins will seep in all the way down to your bones.

Gardevoir

Embrace Pokémon

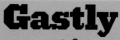

How to Say It: GAR-deh-VWAR
Imperial Height: 5'3"
Metric Height: 1.6 m
Imperial Weight: 106.7 lbs.
Metric Weight: 48.4 kg
Gender: ♂ ♀
Ability: Synchronize / Trace
Weaknesses: Ghost, Steel, Poison

POKÉMON SWORD:
It has the power to predict the future. Its power peaks when it is protecting its Trainer.

POKÉMON SHIELD:
To protect its Trainer, it will expend all its psychic power to create a small black hole.

Ralts   Kirlia   Gardevoir

Gallade

TYPE:
Ghost-Poison

Gastly

Gas Pokémon

How to Say It: GAST-lee
Imperial Height: 4'3"
Metric Height: 1.3 m
Imperial Weight: 0.2 lbs.
Metric Weight: 0.1 kg
Gender: ♂ ♀
Ability: Levitate
Weaknesses: Dark, Ghost, Psychic

POKÉMON SWORD:
Born from gases, anyone would faint if engulfed by its gaseous body, which contains poison.

POKÉMON SHIELD:
With its gas-like body, it can sneak into any place it desires. However, it can be blown away by wind.

Gastly   Haunter   Gengar

Gastrodon

Sea Slug Pokémon

West Sea

How to Say It: GAS-stroh-don
Imperial Height: 2'11"
Metric Height: 0.9 m
Imperial Weight: 65.9 lbs.
Metric Weight: 29.9 kg
Gender: ♂ ♀
Ability: Sticky Hold / Storm Drain
Weaknesses: Grass

POKÉMON SWORD:
It secretes a purple fluid to deter enemies. This fluid isn't poisonous—instead, it's super sticky, and once it sticks, it's very hard to unstick.

POKÉMON SHIELD:
Its body is covered in a sticky slime. It's very susceptible to dehydration, so it can't spend too much time on land.

Shellos ➡ Gastrodon

Gengar
Shadow Pokémon

TYPE:
Ghost-Poison

How to Say It: GHEN-gar
Imperial Height: 4'11"
Metric Height: 1.5 m
Imperial Weight: 89.3 lbs.
Metric Weight: 40.5 kg
Gender: ♂ ♀
Ability: Cursed Body
Weaknesses: Dark, Ghost, Psychic

POKÉMON SWORD:
On the night of a full moon, if shadows move on their own and laugh, it must be Gengar's doing.

POKÉMON SHIELD:
It is said to emerge from darkness to steal the lives of those who become lost in mountains.

 ⇨ ⇨

Gastly　　Haunter　　Gengar

Gigantamax Gengar

Imperial Height: 65'7"+
Metric Height: 20.0 m+
Imperial Weight: ?????.? lbs.
Metric Weight: ?????.? kg

POKÉMON SWORD:
Rumor has it that its gigantic mouth leads not into its body, filled with cursed energy, but instead directly to the afterlife.

POKÉMON SHIELD:
It lays traps, hoping to steal the lives of those it catches. If you stand in front of its mouth, you'll hear your loved ones' voices calling out to you.

Gigalith
Compressed Pokémon

TYPE:
Rock

How to Say It: GIH-gah-lith
Imperial Height: 5'7"
Metric Height: 1.7 m
Imperial Weight: 573.2 lbs.
Metric Weight: 260.0 kg
Gender: ♂ ♀
Ability: Sturdy / Sand Stream
Weaknesses: Water, Grass, Fighting, Ground, Steel

POKÉMON SWORD:
This hardy Pokémon can often be found on construction sites and in mines, working alongside people and Copperajah.

POKÉMON SHIELD:
Although its energy blasts can blow away a dump truck, they have a limitation—they can only be fired when the sun is out.

Roggenrola   Boldore   Gigalith

TYPE:
Ice

Glaceon
Fresh Snow Pokémon

How to Say It: GLAY-cee-on
Imperial Height: 2'7"
Metric Height: 0.8 m
Imperial Weight: 57.1 lbs.
Metric Weight: 25.9 kg
Gender: ♂ ♀
Ability: Snow Cloak
Weaknesses: Fire, Fighting, Rock, Steel

POKÉMON SWORD:
Any who become captivated by the beauty of the snowfall that Glaceon creates will be frozen before they know it.

POKÉMON SHIELD:
The coldness emanating from Glaceon causes powdery snow to form, making it quite a popular Pokémon at ski resorts.

Eevee   Glaceon

Glalie

Face Pokémon

TYPE:
Ice

How to Say It: GLAY-lee
Imperial Height: 4'11"
Metric Height: 1.5 m
Imperial Weight: 565.5 lbs.
Metric Weight: 265.5 kg
Gender: ♂♀
Ability: Inner Focus / Ice Body
Weaknesses: Fire, Fighting, Rock, Steel

POKÉMON SWORD:
It has a body of ice that won't melt, even with fire. It can instantly freeze moisture in the atmosphere.

POKÉMON SHIELD:
It can instantly freeze moisture in the atmosphere. It uses this power to freeze its foes.

Snorunt

Froslass

Glalie

TYPE:
Grass-
Poison

Gloom

Weed Pokémon

How to Say It: GLOOM
Imperial Height: 2'7"
Metric Height: 0.8 m
Imperial Weight: 19.0 lbs.
Metric Weight: 8.6 kg
Gender: ♂♀
Ability: Chlorophyll
Weaknesses: Fire, Flying, Ice, Psychic

POKÉMON SWORD:
Its pistils exude an incredibly foul odor. The horrid stench can cause fainting at a distance of 1.25 miles.

POKÉMON SHIELD:
What appears to be drool is actually sweet honey. It is very sticky and clings stubbornly if touched.

Vileplume

Oddish

Gloom

Bellossom

95

Goldeen

Goldfish Pokémon

How to Say It: GOL-deen
Imperial Height: 2'
Metric Height: 0.6 m
Imperial Weight: 33.1 lbs.
Metric Weight: 15.0 kg
Gender: ♂♀
Ability: Swift Swim / Water Veil
Weaknesses: Electric, Grass

POKÉMON SWORD:
Its dorsal, pectoral, and tail fins wave elegantly in water. That is why it is known as the Water Dancer.

POKÉMON SHIELD:
Its dorsal and pectoral fins are strongly developed like muscles. It can swim at a speed of five knots.

Goldeen   **Seaking**

Golett

Automaton Pokémon

TYPE:
Ground-
Ghost

How to Say It: GO-let
Imperial Height: 3'3"
Metric Height: 1.0 m
Imperial Weight: 202.8 lbs.
Metric Weight: 92.0 kg
Gender: Unknown
Ability: Iron Fist / Klutz
Weaknesses: Water, Grass, Ice, Ghost, Dark

POKÉMON SWORD:
They were sculpted from clay in ancient times. No one knows why, but some of them are driven to continually line up boulders.

POKÉMON SHIELD:
This Pokémon was created from clay. It received orders from its master many thousands of years ago, and it still follows those orders to this day.

Golett   **Golurk**

Golisopod
Hard Scale Pokémon

TYPE:
Bug-
Water

How to Say It: go-LIE-suh-pod
Imperial Height: 6'7"
Metric Height: 2.0 m
Imperial Weight: 238.1 lbs.
Metric Weight: 108.0 kg
Gender: ♂ ♀
Ability: Emergency Exit
Weaknesses: Flying, Electric, Rock

POKÉMON SWORD:
It will do anything to win, taking advantage of every opening and finishing opponents off with the small claws on its front legs.

POKÉMON SHIELD:
They live in sunken ships or in holes in the seabed. When Golisopod and Grapploct battle, the loser becomes the winner's meal.

Wimpod **Golisopod**

Golurk
Automaton Pokémon

TYPE:
Ground-
Ghost

How to Say It: GO-lurk
Imperial Height: 9'2"
Metric Height: 2.8 m
Imperial Weight: 727.5 lbs.
Metric Weight: 330.0 kg
Gender: Unknown
Ability: Iron Fist / Klutz
Weaknesses: Water, Grass, Ice, Ghost, Dark

POKÉMON SWORD:
Artillery platforms built into the walls of ancient castles served as perches from which Golurk could fire energy beams.

POKÉMON SHIELD:
There's a theory that inside Golurk is a perpetual motion machine that produces limitless energy, but this belief hasn't been proven.

Golett **Golurk**

Goodra
Dragon Pokémon

TYPE:
Dragon

How to Say It: GOO-druh
Imperial Height: 6'7"
Metric Height: 2.0 m
Imperial Weight: 331.8 lbs.
Metric Weight: 150.5 kg
Gender: ♂♀
Ability: Sap Sipper / Hydration
Weaknesses: Fairy, Ice, Dragon

POKÉMON SWORD:
Sometimes it misunderstands instructions and appears dazed or bewildered. Many Trainers don't mind, finding this behavior to be adorable.

POKÉMON SHIELD:
Its form of offense is forcefully stretching out its horns. The strikes land 100 times harder than any blow from a heavyweight boxer.

Goomy ⇨ Sliggoo ⇨ Goodra

TYPE:
Dragon

Goomy
Soft Tissue Pokémon

How to Say It: GOO-mee
Imperial Height: 1'
Metric Height: 0.3 m
Imperial Weight: 6.2 lbs.
Metric Weight: 2.8 kg
Gender: ♂♀
Ability: Sap Sipper / Hydration
Weaknesses: Fairy, Ice, Dragon

POKÉMON SWORD:
Because most of its body is water, it will dry up if the weather becomes too arid. It's considered the weakest dragon Pokémon.

POKÉMON SHIELD:
Their horns are powerful sensors. As soon as Goomy pick up any sign of enemies, they go into hiding. This is how they've survived.

Goomy ⇨ Sliggoo ⇨ Goodra

Gossifleur
Flowering Pokémon

How to Say It: GAH-sih-fluhr
Imperial Height: 1'4"
Metric Height: 0.4 m
Imperial Weight: 4.9 lbs.
Metric Weight: 2.2 kg
Gender: ♂ ♀
Ability: Cotton Down / Regenerator
Weaknesses: Fire, Flying, Ice,
    Poison, Bug

POKÉMON SWORD:
It anchors itself in the ground with its single leg, then basks in the sun. After absorbing enough sunlight, its petals spread as it blooms brilliantly.

POKÉMON SHIELD:
It whirls around in the wind while singing a joyous song. This delightful display has charmed many into raising this Pokémon.

Gossifleur   Eldegoss

Gothita
Fixation Pokémon

How to Say It: GAH-THEE-tah
Imperial Height: 1'4"
Metric Height: 0.4 m
Imperial Weight: 12.8 lbs.
Metric Weight: 5.8 kg
Gender: ♂ ♀
Ability: Frisk / Competitive
Weaknesses: Bug, Ghost, Dark

POKÉMON SWORD:
Though they're still only babies, there's psychic power stored in their ribbonlike feelers, and sometimes they use that power to fight.

POKÉMON SHIELD:
Even when nobody seems to be around, Gothita can still be heard making a muted cry. Many believe it's speaking to something only it can see.

Gothita   Gothorita   Gothitelle

Gothitelle

Astral Body Pokémon

How to Say It: GAH-thih-tell
Imperial Height: 4'11"
Metric Height: 1.5 m
Imperial Weight: 97.0 lbs.
Metric Weight: 44.0 kg
Gender: ♂ ♀
Ability: Frisk / Competitive
Weaknesses: Bug, Ghost, Dark

POKÉMON SWORD:
It has tremendous psychic power, but it dislikes conflict. It's also able to predict the future based on the movement of the stars.

POKÉMON SHIELD:
A criminal who was shown his fate by a Gothitelle went missing that same day and was never seen again.

Gothita   Gothorita   Gothitelle

TYPE: Psychic

Gothorita

Manipulate Pokémon

How to Say It: GAH-thoh-REE-tah
Imperial Height: 2'4"
Metric Height: 0.7 m
Imperial Weight: 39.7 lbs.
Metric Weight: 18.0 kg
Gender: ♂ ♀
Ability: Frisk / Competitive
Weaknesses: Bug, Ghost, Dark

POKÉMON SWORD:
It's said that when stars shine in the night sky, this Pokémon will spirit away sleeping children. Some call it the Witch of Punishment.

POKÉMON SHIELD:
On nights when the stars shine, this Pokémon's psychic power is at its strongest. It's unknown just what link Gothorita has to the greater universe.

Gothita   Gothorita   Gothitelle

Gourgeist
Pumpkin Pokémon

How to Say It: GORE-guyst*
(*Rhymes with "heist")
Imperial Height: 2'11"
Metric Height: 0.9 m
Imperial Weight: 27.6 lbs.
Metric Weight: 12.5 kg
Gender: ♂♀
Ability: Pickup / Frisk
Weaknesses: Ghost, Fire, Flying,
Dark, Ice

POKÉMON SWORD:
Eerie cries emanate from its body in the dead of night. The sounds are said to be the wails of spirits who are suffering in the afterlife.

POKÉMON SHIELD:
In the darkness of a new-moon night, Gourgeist will come knocking. Whoever answers the door will be swept off to the afterlife.

Pumpkaboo ⇨ Gourgeist

Grapploct

TYPE:
Fighting

Jujitsu Pokémon

How to Say It: GRAP-lahct
Imperial Height: 5'3"
Metric Height: 1.6 m
Imperial Weight: 86.0 lbs.
Metric Weight: 39.0 kg
Gender: ♂♀
Ability: Limber
Weaknesses: Psychic, Flying, Fairy

POKÉMON SWORD:
A body made up of nothing but muscle makes the grappling moves this Pokémon performs with its tentacles tremendously powerful.

POKÉMON SHIELD:
Searching for an opponent to test its skills against, it emerges onto land. Once the battle is over, it returns to the sea.

Clobbopus ⇨ Grapploct

Greedent

Greedy Pokémon

How to Say It: GREE-dent
Imperial Height: 2'
Metric Height: 0.6 m
Imperial Weight: 13.2 lbs.
Metric Weight: 6.0 kg
Gender: ♂ ♀
Ability: Cheek Pouch
Weaknesses: Fighting

POKÉMON SWORD:
It stashes berries in its tail—so many berries that they fall out constantly. But this Pokémon is a bit slow-witted, so it doesn't notice the loss.

POKÉMON SHIELD:
Common throughout the Galar region, this Pokémon has strong teeth and can chew through the toughest of berry shells.

Skwovet ⇨ Greedent

102

Grimmsnarl

Bulk Up Pokémon

TYPE: Dark-Fairy

How to Say It: GRIM-snarl
Imperial Height: 4'11"
Metric Height: 1.5 m
Imperial Weight: 134.5 lbs.
Metric Weight: 61.0 kg
Gender: ♂
Ability: Prankster / Frisk
Weaknesses: Steel, Fairy, Poison

POKÉMON SWORD:
With the hair wrapped around its body helping to enhance its muscles, this Pokémon can overwhelm even Machamp.

POKÉMON SHIELD:
Its hairs work like muscle fibers. When its hairs unfurl, they latch on to opponents, ensnaring them as tentacles would.

Impidimp   Morgrem   Grimmsnarl

Gigantamax Grimmsnarl

Imperial Height: 105'+
Metric Height: 32.0+ m
Imperial Weight: ????.? lbs.
Metric Weight: ????.? kg

POKÉMON SWORD:
By transforming its leg hair, this Pokémon delivers power-packed drill kicks that can bore huge holes in Galar's terrain.

POKÉMON SHIELD:
Gigantamax energy has caused more hair to sprout all over its body. With the added strength, it can jump over the world's tallest building.

Grookey

Chimp Pokémon

TYPE: Grass

How to Say It: GROO-kee
Imperial Height: 1'
Metric Height: 0.3 m
Imperial Weight: 11.0 lbs.
Metric Weight: 5.0 kg
Gender: ♂ ♀
Ability: Overgrow
Weaknesses: Fire, Flying, Ice, Poison, Bug

POKÉMON SWORD:
When it uses its special stick to strike up a beat, the sound waves produced carry revitalizing energy to the plants and flowers in the area.

POKÉMON SHIELD:
It attacks with rapid beats of its stick. As it strikes with amazing speed, it gets more and more pumped.

Grookey   Thwackey   Rillaboom

Growlithe

TYPE: Fire

Puppy Pokémon

How to Say It: GROWL-lith
Imperial Height: 2'4"
Metric Height: 0.7 m
Imperial Weight: 41.9 lbs
Metric Weight: 19.0 kg
Gender: ♂ ♀
Ability: Intimidate / Flash Fire
Weaknesses: Ground, Rock, Water

POKÉMON SWORD:
It has a brave and trustworthy nature. It fearlessly stands up to bigger and stronger foes.

POKÉMON SHIELD:
Extremely loyal, it will fearlessly bark at any opponent to protect its own Trainer from harm.

Growlithe   Arcanine

Grubbin

Larva Pokémon

How to Say It: GRUB-bin
Imperial Height: 1'4"
Metric Height: 0.4 m
Imperial Weight: 9.7 lbs.
Metric Weight: 4.4 kg
Gender: ♂♀
Ability: Swarm
Weaknesses: Fire, Flying, Rock

POKÉMON SWORD:
Its natural enemies, like Rookidee, may flee rather than risk getting caught in its large mandibles that can snap thick tree branches.

POKÉMON SHIELD:
It uses its big jaws to dig nests into the forest floor, and it loves to feed on sweet tree sap.

Grubbin　Charjabug　Vikavolt

Gurdurr

Muscular Pokémon

How to Say It: GUR-dur
Imperial Height: 3'11"
Metric Height: 1.2 m
Imperial Weight: 88.2 lbs.
Metric Weight: 40.0 kg
Gender: ♂♀
Ability: Guts / Sheer Force
Weaknesses: Flying, Psychic, Fairy

POKÉMON SWORD:
It shows off its muscles to Machoke and other Gurdurr. If it fails to measure up to the other Pokémon, it lies low for a little while.

POKÉMON SHIELD:
Gurdurr excels at demolition—construction is not its forte. In any case, there's skill in the way this Pokémon wields its metal beam.

Timburr　Gurdurr　Conkeldurr

Gyarados

Atrocious Pokémon

TYPE:
Water-Flying

How to Say It: GARE-uh-dos
Imperial Height: 21'4"
Metric Height: 6.5 m
Imperial Weight: 518.1 lbs.
Metric Weight: 235.0 kg
Gender: ♂ ♀
Ability: Intimidate
Weaknesses: Electric, Rock

POKÉMON SWORD:
It has an extremely aggressive nature. The Hyper Beam it shoots from its mouth totally incinerates all targets.

POKÉMON SHIELD:
Once it begins to rampage, a Gyarados will burn everything down, even in a harsh storm.

Magikarp ⇨ Gyarados

Hakamo-o
Scaly Pokémon

TYPE:
Dragon-Fighting

How to Say It: HAH-kah-MOH-oh
Imperial Height: 3'11"
Metric Height: 1.2 m
Imperial Weight: 103.6 lbs.
Metric Weight: 47.0 kg
Gender: ♂ ♀
Ability: Bulletproof / Soundproof
Weaknesses: Fairy, Flying, Psychic, Ice, Dragon

POKÉMON SWORD:
The scaleless, scarred parts of its body are signs of its strength. It shows them off to defeated opponents.

POKÉMON SHIELD:
Before attacking its enemies, it clashes its scales together and roars. Its sharp claws shred the opposition.

Jangmo-o   Hakamo-o   Kommo-o

Hatenna
Calm Pokémon

TYPE:
Psychic

How to Say It: hat-EN-nuh
Imperial Height: 1'4"
Metric Height: 0.4 m
Imperial Weight: 7.5 lbs.
Metric Weight: 3.4 kg
Gender: ♀
Ability: Healer / Anticipation
Weaknesses: Ghost, Dark, Bug

POKÉMON SWORD:
Via the protrusion on its head, it senses other creatures' emotions. If you don't have a calm disposition, it will never warm up to you.

POKÉMON SHIELD:
If this Pokémon senses a strong emotion, it will run away as fast as it can. It prefers areas without people.

Hatenna   Hattrem   Hatterene

Hatterene

Silent Pokémon

How to Say It: HAT-eh-reen
Imperial Height: 6'11"
Metric Height: 2.1 m
Imperial Weight: 11.2 lbs.
Metric Weight: 5.1 kg
Gender: ♀
Ability: Healer / Anticipation
Weaknesses: Ghost, Steel, Poison

POKÉMON SWORD:
It emits psychic power strong enough to cause headaches as a deterrent to the approach of others.

POKÉMON SHIELD:
If you're too loud around it, you risk being torn apart by the claws on its tentacle. This Pokémon is also known as the Forest Witch.

Hatenna   Hattrem   Hatterene

Gigantamax Hatterene

Imperial Height: 85'4"+
Metric Height: 26.0+ m
Imperial Weight: ?????
Metric Weight: ?????. kg

POKÉMON SWORD:
This Pokémon can read the emotions of creatures over 30 miles away. The minute it senses hostility, it goes on the attack.

POKÉMON SHIELD:
Beams like lightning shoot down from its tentacles. It's known to some as the Raging Goddess.

Hattrem

Serene Pokémon

TYPE:
Psychic

How to Say It: HAT-trum
Imperial Height: 2'
Metric Height: 0.6 m
Imperial Weight: 10.6 lbs.
Metric Weight: 4.8 kg
Gender: ♀
Ability: Healer / Anticipation
Weaknesses: Ghost, Dark, Bug

POKÉMON SWORD:
No matter who you are, if you bring strong emotions near this Pokémon, it will silence you violently.

POKÉMON SHIELD:
Using the braids on its head, it pummels foes to get them to quiet down. One blow from those braids would knock out a professional boxer.

Hatenna   Hattrem   Hatterene

Haunter

Gas Pokémon

TYPE:
Ghost-
Poison

How to Say It: HAUNT-ur
Imperial Height: 5'3"
Metric Height: 1.6 m
Imperial Weight: 0.2 lbs.
Metric Weight: 0.1 kg
Gender: ♂ ♀
Ability: Levitate
Weaknesses: Dark, Ghost, Psychic

POKÉMON SWORD:
Its tongue is made of gas. If licked, its victim starts shaking constantly until death eventually comes.

POKÉMON SHIELD:
If you get the feeling of being watched in darkness when nobody is around, Haunter is there.

Gastly   Haunter   Gengar

Hawlucha
Wrestling Pokémon

How to Say It: haw-LOO-cha
Imperial Height: 2'7"
Metric Height: 0.8 m
Imperial Weight: 47.4 lbs.
Metric Weight: 21.5 kg
Gender: ♂ ♀
Ability: Limber / Unburden
Weaknesses: Electric, Psychic, Flying, Ice, Fairy

POKÉMON SWORD:
It drives its opponents to exhaustion with its agile maneuvers, then ends the fight with a flashy finishing move.

POKÉMON SHIELD:
It always strikes a pose before going for its finishing move. Sometimes opponents take advantage of that time to counterattack.

Does not evolve.

TYPE:
Dragon

Haxorus
Axe Jaw Pokémon

How to Say It: HAK-soar-us
Imperial Height: 5'11"
Metric Height: 1.8 m
Imperial Weight: 232.6 lbs.
Metric Weight: 105.5 kg
Gender: ♂ ♀
Ability: Rivalry / Mold Breaker
Weaknesses: Ice, Dragon, Fairy

POKÉMON SWORD:
Its resilient tusks are its pride and joy. It licks up dirt to take in the minerals it needs to keep its tusks in top condition.

POKÉMON SHIELD:
While usually kindhearted, it can be terrifying if angered. Tusks that can slice through steel beams are how Haxorus deals with its adversaries.

Axew   Fraxure   Haxorus

Heatmor

Anteater Pokémon

How to Say It: HEET-mohr
Imperial Height: 4'7"
Metric Height: 1.4 m
Imperial Weight: 127.9 lbs.
Metric Weight: 58.0 kg
Gender: ♂ ♀
Ability: Gluttony / Flash Fire
Weaknesses: Water, Ground, Rock

POKÉMON SWORD:
There's a hole in its tail that allows it to draw in the air it needs to keep its fire burning. If the hole gets blocked, this Pokémon will fall ill.

POKÉMON SHIELD:
A flame serves as its tongue, melting through the hard shell of Durant so that Heatmor can devour their insides.

Does not evolve.

Heliolisk

Generator Pokémon

TYPE:
Electric-
Normal

How to Say It: HEE-lee-oh-lisk
Imperial Height: 3'3"
Metric Height: 1.0 m
Imperial Weight: 46.3 lbs.
Metric Weight: 21.0 kg
Gender: ♂ ♀
Ability: Dry Skin / Sand Veil
Weaknesses: Fighting, Ground

POKÉMON SWORD:
A now-vanished desert culture treasured these Pokémon. Appropriately, when Heliolisk came to the Galar region, treasure came with them.

POKÉMON SHIELD:
One Heliolisk basking in the sun with its frill outspread is all it would take to produce enough electricity to power a city.

Helioptile **Heliolisk**

Helioptile
Generator Pokémon

How to Say It: hee-lee-AHP-tile
Imperial Height: 1'8"
Metric Height: 0.5 m
Imperial Weight: 13.2 lbs.
Metric Weight: 6.0 kg
Gender: ♂ ♀
Ability: Dry Skin / Sand Veil
Weaknesses: Fighting, Ground

POKÉMON SWORD:
When spread, the frills on its head act like solar panels, generating the power behind this Pokémon's electric moves.

POKÉMON SHIELD:
The sun powers this Pokémon's electricity generation. Interruption of that process stresses Helioptile to the point of weakness.

Helioptile   Heliolisk

TYPE:
Ground

Hippopotas
Hippo Pokémon

How to Say It: HIP-poh-puh-TOSS
Imperial Height: 2'7"
Metric Height: 0.8 m
Imperial Weight: 109.1 lbs.
Metric Weight: 49.5 kg
Gender: ♂ ♀
Ability: Sand Stream
Weaknesses: Grass, Ice, Water

POKÉMON SWORD:
It moves through the sands with its mouth open, swallowing sand along with its prey. It gets rid of the sand by spouting it from its nose.

POKÉMON SHIELD:
This Pokémon is active during the day and passes the cold desert nights burrowed snugly into the sand.

Hippopotas   Hippowdon

Hippowdon
Heavyweight Pokémon

TYPE: Ground

How to Say It: hip-POW-don
Imperial Height: 6'7"
Metric Height: 2.0 m
Imperial Weight: 661.4 lbs.
Metric Weight: 300.0 kg
Gender: ♂ ♀
Ability: Sand Stream
Weaknesses: Grass, Ice, Water

POKÉMON SWORD:
Stones can get stuck in the ports on their bodies. Dwebble help dislodge such stones, so Hippowdon look after these Pokémon.

POKÉMON SHIELD:
When roused to violence by its rage, it spews out the quantities of sand it has swallowed and whips up a sandstorm.

Hippopotas   Hippowdon

Hitmonchan
Punching Pokémon

TYPE: Fighting

How to Say It: HIT-mon-CHAN
Imperial Height: 4'7"
Metric Height: 1.4 m
Imperial Weight: 110.7 lbs.
Metric Weight: 50.2 kg
Gender: ♂
Ability: Keen Eye / Iron Fist
Weaknesses: Flying, Psychic, Fairy

POKÉMON SWORD:
Its punches slice the air. They are launched at such high speed, even a slight graze could cause a burn.

POKÉMON SHIELD:
Its punches slice the air. However, it seems to need a short break after fighting for three minutes.

Hitmonlee

Tyrogue

Hitmonchan

Hitmontop

Hitmonlee

Kicking Pokémon

TYPE:
Fighting

How to Say It: HIT-mon-LEE
Imperial Height: 4'11"
Metric Height: 1.5 m
Imperial Weight: 109.8 lbs.
Metric Weight: 49.8 kg
Gender: ♂
Ability: Limber / Reckless
Weaknesses: Flying, Psychic, Fairy

Tyrogue → Hitmonchan → Hitmonlee / Hitmontop

POKÉMON SWORD:
This amazing Pokémon has an awesome sense of balance. It can kick in succession from any position.

POKÉMON SHIELD:
The legs freely contract and stretch. The stretchy legs allow it to hit a distant foe with a rising kick.

Hitmontop

Handstand Pokémon

TYPE:
Fighting

How to Say It: HIT-mon-TOP
Imperial Height: 4'7"
Metric Height: 1.4 m
Imperial Weight: 105.8 lbs.
Metric Weight: 48.0 kg
Gender: ♂
Ability: Intimidate / Technician
Weaknesses: Flying, Psychic, Fairy

Tyrogue → Hitmonchan → Hitmonlee / Hitmontop

POKÉMON SWORD:
It launches kicks while spinning. If it spins at high speed, it may bore its way into the ground.

POKÉMON SHIELD:
After doing a handstand to throw off the opponent's timing, it presents its fancy kick moves.

Honedge
Sword Pokémon

TYPE: Steel-Ghost

How to Say It: HONE-ej
Imperial Height: 2'7"
Metric Height: 0.8 m
Imperial Weight: 4.4 lbs.
Metric Weight: 2.0 kg
Gender: ♂♀
Ability: No Guard
Weaknesses: Fire, Ghost, Dark, Ground

POKÉMON SWORD:
Honedge's soul once belonged to a person who was killed a long time ago by the sword that makes up Honedge's body.

POKÉMON SHIELD:
The blue eye on the sword's handguard is the true body of Honedge. With its old cloth, it drains people's lives away.

Honedge   Doublade   Aegislash

Hoothoot
Owl Pokémon

TYPE: Normal-Flying

How to Say It: HOOT-HOOT
Imperial Height: 2'4"
Metric Height: 0.7 m
Imperial Weight: 46.7 lbs.
Metric Weight: 21.2 kg
Gender: ♂♀
Ability: Insomnia / Keen Eye
Weaknesses: Electric, Ice, Rock

POKÉMON SWORD:
It always stands on one foot. It changes feet so fast, the movement can rarely be seen.

POKÉMON SHIELD:
It begins to hoot at the same time every day. Some Trainers use them in place of clocks.

Hoothoot   Noctowl

Hydreigon
Brutal Pokémon

TYPE:
Dark-Dragon

How to Say It: hy-DRY-guhn
Imperial Height: 5'11"
Metric Height: 1.8 m
Imperial Weight: 352.7 lbs.
Metric Weight: 160.0 kg
Gender: ♂ ♀
Ability: Levitate
Weaknesses: Ice, Fighting, Bug, Dragon, Fairy

POKÉMON SWORD:
There are a slew of stories about villages that were destroyed by Hydreigon. It bites anything that moves.

POKÉMON SHIELD:
The three heads take turns sinking their teeth into the opponent. Their attacks won't slow until their target goes down.

Deino Zweilous Hydreigon

TYPE:
Dark-Fairy

Impidimp
Wily Pokémon

How to Say It: IMP-ih-dimp
Imperial Height: 1'4"
Metric Height: 0.4 m
Imperial Weight: 12.1 lbs.
Metric Weight: 5.5 kg
Gender: ♂
Ability: Prankster / Frisk
Weaknesses: Steel, Fairy, Poison

POKÉMON SWORD:
Through its nose, it sucks in the emanations produced by people and Pokémon when they feel annoyed. It thrives off this negative energy.

POKÉMON SHIELD:
It sneaks into people's homes, stealing things and feasting on the negative energy of the frustrated occupants.

Impidimp Morgrem Grimmsnarl

Indeedee
Emotion Pokémon

Male Form

Female Form

How to Say It: in-DEE-dee
Imperial Height: 2'11"
Metric Height: 0.9 m
Imperial Weight: 61.7 lbs.
Metric Weight: 28.0 kg
Gender: ♂ ♀
Ability: Synchronize / Inner Focus (Male) / Own Tempo (Female)
Weaknesses: Dark, Bug

MALE

POKÉMON SWORD:
It uses the horns on its head to sense the emotions of others. Males will act as valets for those they serve, looking after their every need.

POKÉMON SHIELD:
Through its horns, it can pick up on the emotions of creatures around it. Positive emotions are the source of its strength.

FEMALE

POKÉMON SWORD:
These intelligent Pokémon touch horns with each other to share information between them.

POKÉMON SHIELD:
They diligently serve people and Pokémon so they can gather feelings of gratitude. The females are particularly good at babysitting.

Does not evolve

Inkay

Revolving Pokémon

How to Say It: in-KAY
Imperial Height: 1'4"
Metric Height: 0.4 m
Imperial Weight: 7.7 lbs.
Metric Weight: 3.5 kg
Gender: ♂ ♀
Ability: Contrary / Suction Cups
Weaknesses: Fairy, Bug

POKÉMON SWORD:
It spins while making its luminescent spots flash. These spots allow it to communicate with others by using different patterns of light.

POKÉMON SHIELD:
By exposing foes to the blinking of its luminescent spots, Inkay demoralizes them, and then it seizes the chance to flee.

Inkay ⇨ Malamar

Inteleon

Secret Agent Pokémon

TYPE: Water

How to Say It: in-TELL-ee-un
Imperial Height: 6'3"
Metric Height: 1.9 m
Imperial Weight: 99.6 lbs.
Metric Weight: 45.2 kg
Gender: ♂ ♀
Ability: Torrent
Weaknesses: Grass, Electric

POKÉMON SWORD:
It has many hidden capabilities, such as fingertips that can shoot water and a membrane on its back that it can use to glide through the air.

POKÉMON SHIELD:
Its nictitating membranes let it pick out foes' weak points so it can precisely blast them with water that shoots from its fingertips at Mach 3.

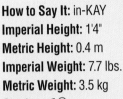

Sobble ⇨ Drizzile ⇨ Inteleon

118

Jangmo-o
Scaly Pokémon

How to Say It: JANG-MOH-oh
Imperial Height: 2'
Metric Height: 0.6 m
Imperial Weight: 65.5 lbs.
Metric Weight: 29.7 kg
Gender: ♂ ♀
Ability: Bulletproof / Soundproof
Weaknesses: Fairy, Ice, Dragon

POKÉMON SWORD:
They learn to fight by smashing their head scales together. The dueling strengthens both their skills and their spirits.

POKÉMON SHIELD:
Jangmo-o strikes its scales to communicate with others of its kind. Its scales are actually fur that's become as hard as metal.

Jangmo-o ⇨ Hakamo-o ⇨ Kommo-o

Jellicent
Floating Pokémon

How to Say It: JEL-ih-sent
Imperial Height: 7'3"
Metric Height: 2.2 m
Imperial Weight: 297.6 lbs.
Metric Weight: 135.0 kg
Gender: ♂ ♀
Ability: Water Absorb / Cursed Body
Weaknesses: Grass, Electric, Ghost, Dark

Male Form

Female Form

MALE

POKÉMON SWORD:
Most of this Pokémon's body composition is identical to sea water. It makes sunken ships its lair.

POKÉMON SHIELD:
Whenever a full moon hangs in the night sky, schools of Jellicent gather near the surface of the sea, waiting for their prey to appear.

Frillish **Jellicent**

FEMALE

POKÉMON SWORD:
These Pokémon have body compositions that are mostly identical to seawater. They make their lairs from sunken ships.

POKÉMON SHIELD:
The crown on its head gets bigger and bigger as it absorbs more and more of the life-force of other creatures.

Jolteon
Lightning Pokémon

How to Say It: JOL-tee-on
Imperial Height: 2'7"
Metric Height: 0.8 m
Imperial Weight: 54.0 lbs.
Metric Weight: 24.5 kg
Gender: ♂ ♀
Ability: Volt Absorb
Weaknesses: Ground

Eevee **Jolteon**

POKÉMON SWORD:
If it is angered or startled, the fur all over its body bristles like sharp needles that pierce foes.

POKÉMON SHIELD:
It accumulates negative ions in the atmosphere to blast out 10,000-volt lightning bolts.

Joltik
Attaching Pokémon

How to Say It: JOHL-tik
Imperial Height: 4"
Metric Height: 0.1 m
Imperial Weight: 1.3 lbs.
Metric Weight: 0.6 kg
Gender: ♂ ♀
Ability: Compound Eyes / Unnerve
Weaknesses: Fire, Rock

POKÉMON SWORD:
Joltik can be found clinging to other Pokémon. It's soaking up static electricity because it can't produce a charge on its own.

POKÉMON SHIELD:
Joltik latch on to other Pokémon and suck out static electricity. They're often found sticking to Yamper's hindquarters.

Joltik   Galvantula

Karrablast
Clamping Pokémon

How to Say It: KAIR-ruh-blast
Imperial Height: 1'8"
Metric Height: 0.5 m
Imperial Weight: 13.0 lbs.
Metric Weight: 5.9 kg
Gender: ♂ ♀
Ability: Swarm / Shed Skin
Weaknesses: Fire, Flying, Rock

POKÉMON SWORD:
Its strange physiology reacts to electrical energy in interesting ways. The presence of a Shelmet will cause this Pokémon to evolve.

POKÉMON SHIELD:
It spits a liquid from its mouth to melt through Shelmet's shell. Karrablast doesn't eat the shell—it eats only the contents.

Karrablast   Escavalier

Kingler
Pincer Pokémon

TYPE: Water

How to Say It: KING-lur
Imperial Height: 4'3"
Metric Height: 1.3 m
Imperial Weight: 132.3 lbs.
Metric Weight: 60.0 kg
Gender: ♂ ♀
Ability: Hyper Cutter / Shell Armor
Weaknesses: Electric, Grass

POKÉMON SWORD:
Its large and hard pincer has 10,000-horsepower strength. However, being so big, it is unwieldy to move.

POKÉMON SHIELD:
Its oversized claw is very powerful, but when it's not in battle, the claw just gets in the way.

Krabby **Kingler**

Gigantamax Kingler

Imperial Height: 62'4"+
Metric Height: 19.0+ m
Imperial Weight: ?????.? lbs.
Metric Weight: ?????.? kg

POKÉMON SWORD:
The flow of Gigantamax energy has spurred this Pokémon's left pincer to grow to an enormous size. That claw can pulverize anything.

POKÉMON SHIELD:
The bubbles it spews out are strongly alkaline. Any opponents hit by them will have their bodies quickly melted away.

Kirlia

Emotion Pokémon

How to Say It: KERL-lee-ah
Imperial Height: 2'7"
Metric Height: 0.8 m
Imperial Weight: 44.5 lbs.
Metric Weight: 20.2 kg
Gender: ♂ ♀
Ability: Synchronize / Trace
Weaknesses: Ghost, Steel, Poison

POKÉMON SWORD:
If its Trainer becomes happy, it overflows with energy, dancing joyously while spinning about.

POKÉMON SHIELD:
It has a psychic power that enables it to distort the space around it and see into the future.

Gardevoir

Ralts   Kirlia

Gallade

Klang

Gear Pokémon

How to Say It: KLANG
Imperial Height: 2'
Metric Height: 0.6 m
Imperial Weight: 112.4 lbs.
Metric Weight: 51.0 kg
Gender: Unknown
Ability: Plus / Minus
Weaknesses: Fire, Fighting, Ground

POKÉMON SWORD:
When Klang goes all out, the minigear links up perfectly with the outer part of the big gear, and this Pokémon's rotation speed increases sharply.

POKÉMON SHIELD:
Many companies in the Galar region choose Klang as their logo. This Pokémon is considered the symbol of industrial technology.

Klink

Klang

Klinklang

Klink
Gear Pokémon

How to Say It: KLEENK
Imperial Height: 1'
Metric Height: 0.3 m
Imperial Weight: 46.3 lbs.
Metric Weight: 21.0 kg
Gender: Unknown
Ability: Plus / Minus
Weaknesses: Fire, Fighting, Ground

POKÉMON SWORD:
The two minigears that compose this Pokémon are closer than twins. They mesh well only with each other.

POKÉMON SHIELD:
It's suspected that Klink were the inspiration behind ancient people's invention of the first gears.

Klink   Klang   Klinklang

Klinklang
Gear Pokémon

TYPE:
Steel

How to Say It: KLEENK-klang
Imperial Height: 2'
Metric Height: 0.6 m
Imperial Weight: 178.6 lbs.
Metric Weight: 81.0 kg
Gender: Unknown
Ability: Plus / Minus
Weaknesses: Fire, Fighting, Ground

POKÉMON SWORD:
From its spikes, it launches powerful blasts of electricity. Its red core contains an enormous amount of energy.

POKÉMON SHIELD:
The three gears that compose this Pokémon spin at high speed. Its new spiked gear isn't a living creature.

Klink   Klang   Klinklang

Koffing

Poison Gas Pokémon

TYPE:
Poison

How to Say It: KOFF-ing
Imperial Height: 2'
Metric Height: 0.6 m
Imperial Weight: 2.2 lbs.
Metric Weight: 1.0 kg
Gender: ♂ ♀
Ability: Levitate / Neutralizing Gas
Weaknesses: Psychic

POKÉMON SWORD:
Its body is full of poisonous gas. It floats into garbage dumps, seeking out the fumes of raw, rotting trash.

POKÉMON SHIELD:
It adores polluted air. Some claim that Koffing used to be more plentiful in the Galar region than they are now.

Koffing   **Galarian Weezing**

TYPE:
Dragon-Fighting

Kommo-o

Scaly Pokémon

How to Say It: koh-MOH-oh
Imperial Height: 5'3"
Metric Height: 1.6 m
Imperial Weight: 172.4 lbs.
Metric Weight: 78.2 kg
Gender: ♂ ♀
Ability: Bulletproof / Soundproof
Weaknesses: Fairy, Flying, Psychic, Ice, Dragon

POKÉMON SWORD:
It clatters its tail scales to unnerve opponents. This Pokémon will battle only those who stand steadfast in the face of this display.

POKÉMON SHIELD:
Certain ruins have paintings of ancient warriors wearing armor made of Kommo-o scales.

ngmo-o   Hakamo-o   Kommo-o

Krabby
River Crab Pokémon

How to Say It: KRAB-ee
Imperial Height: 1'4"
Metric Height: 0.4 m
Imperial Weight: 14.3 lbs.
Metric Weight: 6.5 kg
Gender: ♂ ♀
Ability: Hyper Cutter / Shell Armor
Weaknesses: Electric, Grass

POKÉMON SWORD:
It can be found near the sea. The large pincers grow back if they are torn out of their sockets.

POKÉMON SHIELD:
If it senses danger approaching, it cloaks itself with bubbles from its mouth so it will look bigger.

Krabby   **Kingler**

Lampent
Lamp Pokémon

How to Say It: LAM-pent
Imperial Height: 2'
Metric Height: 0.6 m
Imperial Weight: 28.7 lbs.
Metric Weight: 13.0 kg
Gender: ♂ ♀
Ability: Flash Fire / Flame Body
Weaknesses: Water, Ground, Rock, Ghost, Dark

POKÉMON SWORD:
This Pokémon appears just before someone passes away, so it's feared as an emissary of death.

POKÉMON SHIELD:
It lurks in cities, pretending to be a lamp. Once it finds someone whose death is near, it will trail quietly after them.

Litwick   **Lampent**   **Chandelure**

TYPE:
Water-
Electric

Lanturn
Light Pokémon

How to Say It: LAN-turn
Imperial Height: 3'11"
Metric Height: 1.2 m
Imperial Weight: 49.6 lbs.
Metric Weight: 22.5 kg
Gender: ♂ ♀
Ability: Volt Absorb / Illuminate
Weaknesses: Grass, Ground

POKÉMON SWORD:
The light it emits is so bright that it can illuminate the sea's surface from a depth of over three miles.

POKÉMON SHIELD:
This Pokémon flashes a bright light that blinds its prey. This creates an opening for it to deliver an electrical attack.

Chinchou ⇨ Lanturn

127

Lapras

Transport Pokémon

How to Say It: LAP-rus
Imperial Height: 8'2"
Metric Height: 2.5 m
Imperial Weight: 485.0 lbs.
Metric Weight: 220.0 kg
Gender: ♂♀
Ability: Water Absorb / Shell Armor
Weaknesses: Electric, Fighting, Grass, Rock

POKÉMON SWORD:
A smart and kindhearted Pokémon, it glides across the surface of the sea while its beautiful song echoes around it.

POKÉMON SHIELD:
Crossing icy seas is no issue for this cold-resistant Pokémon. Its smooth skin is a little cool to the touch.

Does not evolve.

Gigantamax Lapras

Imperial Height: 78'9"+
Metric Height: 24.0+ m
Imperial Weight: ?????.? lbs.
Metric Weight: ?????.? kg

POKÉMON SWORD:
Over 5,000 people can ride on its shell at once. And it's a very comfortable ride, without the slightest shaking or swaying.

POKÉMON SHIELD:
It surrounds itself with a huge ring of gathered ice particles. It uses the ring to smash any icebergs that might impede its graceful swimming.

Larvitar
Rock Skin Pokémon

TYPE:
Rock-
Ground

How to Say It: LAR-vuh-tar
Imperial Height: 2'
Metric Height: 0.6 m
Imperial Weight: 158.7 lbs.
Metric Weight: 72.0 kg
Gender: ♂♀
Ability: Guts
Weaknesses: Grass, Water, Fighting, Ground, Ice, Steel

POKÉMON SWORD:
Born deep underground, it comes aboveground and becomes a pupa once it has finished eating the surrounding soil.

POKÉMON SHIELD:
It feeds on soil. After it has eaten a large mountain, it will fall asleep so it can grow.

Larvitar   Pupitar   Tyranitar

Leafeon
Verdant Pokémon

TYPE:
Grass

How to Say It: LEAF-ee-on
Imperial Height: 3'3"
Metric Height: 1.0 m
Imperial Weight: 56.2 lbs.
Metric Weight: 25.5 kg
Gender: ♂♀
Ability: Leaf Guard
Weaknesses: Bug, Fire, Flying, Ice, Poison

POKÉMON SWORD:
Galarians favor the distinctive aroma that drifts from this Pokémon's leaves. There's a popular perfume made using that scent.

POKÉMON SHIELD:
This Pokémon's tail is blade sharp, with a fantastic cutting edge that can slice right though large trees.

Eevee   Leafeon

Liepard
Cruel Pokémon

TYPE:
Dark

How to Say It: LY-purd
Imperial Height: 3'7"
Metric Height: 1.1 m
Imperial Weight: 82.7 lbs.
Metric Weight: 37.5 kg
Gender: ♂ ♀
Ability: Limber / Unburden
Weaknesses: Fighting, Bug, Fairy

POKÉMON SWORD:
Don't be fooled by its gorgeous fur and elegant figure. This is a moody and vicious Pokémon.

POKÉMON SHIELD:
This stealthy Pokémon sneaks up behind prey without making any sound at all. It competes with Thievul for territory.

Purrloin ⇨ **Liepard**

GALARIAN
Linoone
Rushing Pokémon

TYPE:
Dark-
Normal

How to Say It: line-NOON
Imperial Height: 1'8"
Metric Height: 0.5 m
Imperial Weight: 71.7 lbs.
Metric Weight: 32.5 kg
Gender: ♂ ♀
Ability: Pickup / Gluttony
Weaknesses: Fairy, Bug, Fighting

POKÉMON SWORD:
Once the opposition is enraged, this Pokémon hurls itself at the opponent, tackling them forcefully.

POKÉMON SHIELD:
This very aggressive Pokémon will recklessly challenge opponents stronger than itself.

Galarian Zigzagoon ⇨ **Galarian Linoone** ⇨ **Obstagoon**

Litwick

Candle Pokémon

How to Say It: LIT-wik
Imperial Height: 1'
Metric Height: 0.3 m
Imperial Weight: 6.8 lbs.
Metric Weight: 3.1 kg
Gender: ♂ ♀
Ability: Flash Fire / Flame Body
Weaknesses: Water, Ground, Rock, Ghost, Dark

POKÉMON SWORD:
The flame on its head keeps its body slightly warm. This Pokémon takes lost children by the hand to guide them to the spirit world.

POKÉMON SHIELD:
The younger the life this Pokémon absorbs, the brighter and eerier the flame on its head burns.

Litwick   Lampent   Chandelure

TYPE:
Water-Grass

Lombre

Jolly Pokémon

How to Say It: LOM-brey
Imperial Height: 3'11"
Metric Height: 1.2 m
Imperial Weight: 71.6 lbs.
Metric Weight: 32.5 kg
Gender: ♂ ♀
Ability: Swift Swim / Rain Dish
Weaknesses: Bug, Flying, Poison

POKÉMON SWORD:
It is nocturnal and becomes active at nightfall. It feeds on aquatic mosses that grow in the riverbed.

POKÉMON SHIELD:
It lives at the water's edge where it is sunny. It sleeps on a bed of water grass by day and becomes active at night.

Lotad   Lombre   Ludicolo

Lotad
Water Weed Pokémon

How to Say It: LOW-tad
Imperial Height: 1'8"
Metric Height: 0.5 m
Imperial Weight: 5.7 lbs.
Metric Weight: 2.6 kg
Gender: ♂ ♀
Ability: Swift Swim / Rain Dish
Weaknesses: Bug, Flying, Poison

POKÉMON SWORD:
It searches about for clean water. If it does not drink water for too long, the leaf on its head wilts.

POKÉMON SHIELD:
Its leaf grew too large for it to live on land. That is how it began to live floating in the water.

Lotad ⇨ Lombre ⇨ Ludicolo

Lucario
Aura Pokémon

How to Say It: loo-CAR-ee-oh
Imperial Height: 3'11"
Metric Height: 1.2 m
Imperial Weight: 119.0 lbs.
Metric Weight: 54.0 kg
Gender: ♂ ♀
Ability: Steadfast / Inner Focus
Weaknesses: Fighting, Fire, Ground

POKÉMON SWORD:
It controls waves known as auras, which are powerful enough to pulverize huge rocks. It uses these waves to take down its prey.

POKÉMON SHIELD:
It can tell what people are thinking. Only Trainers who have justice in their hearts can earn this Pokémon's trust.

Riolu ⇨ Lucario

Ludicolo

Carefree Pokémon

How to Say It: LOO-dee-KO-low
Imperial Height: 4'11"
Metric Height: 1.5 m
Imperial Weight: 121.3 lbs.
Metric Weight: 55.0 kg
Gender: ♂♀
Ability: Swift Swim / Rain Dish
Weaknesses: Bug, Flying, Poison

POKÉMON SWORD:
The rhythm of bright, festive music activates Ludicolo's cells, making it more powerful.

POKÉMON SHIELD:
If it hears festive music, it begins moving in rhythm in order to amplify its power.

Lotad   Lombre   Ludicolo

Lunatone

Meteorite Pokémon

TYPE:
Rock-
Psychic

How to Say It: LOO-nuh-tone
Imperial Height: 3'3"
Metric Height: 1.0 m
Imperial Weight: 370.4 lbs.
Metric Weight: 168.0 kg
Gender: Unknown
Ability: Levitate
Weaknesses: Bug, Dark, Ghost, Grass,
Steel, Water

POKÉMON SWORD:
The phase of the moon apparently has some effect on its power. It's active on the night of a full moon.

POKÉMON SHIELD:
It was discovered at the site of a meteor strike 40 years ago. Its stare can lull its foes to sleep.

Does not evolve.

Machamp
Superpower Pokémon

TYPE: Fighting

How to Say It: muh-CHAMP
Imperial Height: 5'3"
Metric Height: 1.6 m
Imperial Weight: 286.6 lbs.
Metric Weight: 130.0 kg
Gender: ♂ ♀
Ability: Guts / No Guard
Weaknesses: Flying, Psychic, Fairy

POKÉMON SWORD:
It quickly swings its four arms to rock its opponents with ceaseless punches and chops from all angles.

POKÉMON SHIELD:
With four arms that react more quickly than it can think, it can execute many punches at once.

Machop   Machoke   Machamp

Gigantamax Machamp

Imperial Height: 82'+
Metric Height: 25.0+ m
Imperial Weight: ?????? lbs.
Metric Weight: ?????? kg

POKÉMON SWORD:
The Gigantamax energy coursing through its arms makes its punches hit as hard as bomb blasts.

POKÉMON SHIELD:
One of these Pokémon once used its immeasurable strength to lift a large ship that was in trouble. It then carried the ship to port.

Machoke
Superpower Pokémon

TYPE:
Fighting

How to Say It: muh-CHOKE
Imperial Height: 4'11"
Metric Height: 1.5 m
Imperial Weight: 155.4 lbs.
Metric Weight: 70.5 kg
Gender: ♂♀
Ability: Guts / No Guard
Weaknesses: Flying, Psychic, Fairy

POKÉMON SWORD:
Its muscular body is so powerful, it must wear a power-save belt to be able to regulate its motions.

POKÉMON SHIELD:
Its formidable body never gets tired. It helps people by doing work such as the moving of heavy goods.

Machop Machoke Machamp

TYPE:
Fighting

Machop
Superpower Pokémon

How to Say It: muh-CHOP
Imperial Height: 2'7"
Metric Height: 0.8 m
Imperial Weight: 43.0 lbs.
Metric Weight: 19.5 kg
Gender: ♂♀
Ability: Guts / No Guard
Weaknesses: Flying, Psychic, Fairy

POKÉMON SWORD:
Its whole body is composed of muscles. Even though it's the size of a human child, it can hurl 100 grown-ups.

POKÉMON SHIELD:
Always brimming with power, it passes time by lifting boulders. Doing so makes it even stronger.

Machop Machoke Machamp

Magikarp
Fish Pokémon

How to Say It: MADGE-eh-karp
Imperial Height: 2'11"
Metric Height: 0.9 m
Imperial Weight: 22.0 lbs.
Metric Weight: 10.0 kg
Gender: ♂ ♀
Ability: Swift Swim
Weaknesses: Electric, Grass

POKÉMON SWORD:
It is virtually worthless in terms of both power and speed. It is the most weak and pathetic Pokémon in the world.

POKÉMON SHIELD:
This weak and pathetic Pokémon gets easily pushed along rivers when there are strong currents.

Magikarp   Gyarados

Malamar
Overturning Pokémon

How to Say It: MAL-uh-MAR
Imperial Height: 4'11"
Metric Height: 1.5 m
Imperial Weight: 103.6 lbs.
Metric Weight: 47.0 kg
Gender: ♂ ♀
Ability: Contrary / Suction Cups
Weaknesses: Fairy, Bug

POKÉMON SWORD:
Gazing at its luminescent spots will quickly induce a hypnotic state, putting the observer under Malamar's control.

POKÉMON SHIELD:
It's said that Malamar's hypnotic powers played a role in certain history-changing events.

Inkay   Malamar

Mamoswine

Twin Tusk Pokémon

TYPE: Ice-Ground

How to Say It: MAM-oh-swine
Imperial Height: 8'2"
Metric Height: 2.5 m
Imperial Weight: 641.5 lbs.
Metric Weight: 291.0 kg
Gender: ♂ ♀
Ability: Oblivious / Snow Cloak
Weaknesses: Fighting, Fire, Grass, Steel, Water

POKÉMON SWORD:
This Pokémon can be spotted in wall paintings from as far back as 10,000 years ago. For a while, it was thought to have gone extinct.

POKÉMON SHIELD:
It looks strong, and that's exactly what it is. As the weather grows colder, its ice tusks grow longer, thicker, and more impressive.

Swinub   Piloswine   Mamoswine

Mandibuzz

Bone Vulture Pokémon

TYPE: Dark-Flying

How to Say It: MAN-dih-buz
Imperial Height: 3'11"
Metric Height: 1.2 m
Imperial Weight: 87.1 lbs.
Metric Weight: 39.5 kg
Gender: ♀
Ability: Big Pecks / Overcoat
Weaknesses: Electric, Ice, Rock, Fairy

POKÉMON SWORD:
Although it's a bit of a ruffian, this Pokémon will take lost Vullaby under its wing and care for them till they're ready to leave the nest.

POKÉMON SHIELD:
They adorn themselves with bones. There seem to be fashion trends among them, as different bones come into and fall out of popularity.

Vullaby   Mandibuzz

Manectric

Discharge Pokémon

TYPE:
Electric

How to Say It: mane-EK-trick
Imperial Height: 4'11"
Metric Height: 1.5 m
Imperial Weight: 88.6 lbs.
Metric Weight: 40.2 kg
Gender: ♂ ♀
Ability: Static / Lightning Rod
Weaknesses: Ground

POKÉMON SWORD:
It stimulates its own muscles with electricity, so it can move quickly. It eases its soreness with electricity, too, so it can recover quickly as well.

POKÉMON SHIELD:
It rarely appears before people. It is said to nest where lightning has fallen.

Electrike **Manectric**

TYPE:
Water-
Flying

Mantine

Kite Pokémon

How to Say It: MAN-teen
Imperial Height: 6'11"
Metric Height: 2.1 m
Imperial Weight: 485.0 lbs.
Metric Weight: 220.0 kg
Gender: ♂ ♀
Ability: Swift Swim / Water Absorb
Weaknesses: Electric, Rock

POKÉMON SWORD:
If it builds up enough speed swimming, it can jump out above the waves and glide for over 300 feet.

POKÉMON SHIELD:
As it majestically swims, it doesn't care if Remoraid attach to it to scavenge for its leftovers.

Mantyke **Mantine**

Mantyke
Kite Pokémon

TYPE:
Water-
Flying

How to Say It: MAN-tike
Imperial Height: 3'3"
Metric Height: 1.0 m
Imperial Weight: 143.3 lbs.
Metric Weight: 65.0 kg
Gender: ♂♀
Ability: Swift Swim / Water Absorb
Weaknesses: Electric, Rock

POKÉMON SWORD:
Mantyke living in Galar seem to be somewhat sluggish. The colder waters of the seas in this region may be the cause.

POKÉMON SHIELD:
It swims along with a school of Remoraid, and they'll all fight together to repel attackers.

Mantyke   ⇨   Mantine

Maractus
Cactus Pokémon

TYPE:
Grass

How to Say It: mah-RAK-tus
Imperial Height: 3'3"
Metric Height: 1.0 m
Imperial Weight: 61.7 lbs.
Metric Weight: 28.0 kg
Gender: ♂♀
Ability: Water Absorb / Chlorophyll
Weaknesses: Fire, Ice, Poison, Flying, Bug

POKÉMON SWORD:
With noises that could be mistaken for the rattles of maracas, it creates an upbeat rhythm, startling bird Pokémon and making them fly off in a hurry.

POKÉMON SHIELD:
Once each year, this Pokémon scatters its seeds. They're jam-packed with nutrients, making them a precious food source out in the desert.

Does not evolve.

Mareanie

Brutal Star Pokémon

TYPE:
Poison-
Water

How to Say It: muh-REE-nee
Imperial Height: 1'4"
Metric Height: 0.4 m
Imperial Weight: 17.6 lbs.
Metric Weight: 8.0 kg
Gender: ♂♀
Ability: Merciless / Limber
Weaknesses: Psychic, Electric, Ground

POKÉMON SWORD:
The first symptom of its sting is numbness. The next is an itching sensation so intense that it's impossible to resist the urge to claw at your skin.

POKÉMON SHIELD:
Unlike their Alolan counterparts, the Mareanie of the Galar region have not yet figured out that the branches of Corsola are delicious.

Mareanie → Toxapex

Mawile

Deceiver Pokémon

TYPE:
Steel-
Fairy

How to Say It: MAW-while
Imperial Height: 2'
Metric Height: 0.6 m
Imperial Weight: 25.4 lbs.
Metric Weight: 11.5 kg
Gender: ♂♀
Ability: Hyper Cutter / Intimidate
Weaknesses: Fire, Ground

POKÉMON SWORD:
It uses its docile-looking face to lull foes into complacency, then bites with its huge, relentless jaws.

POKÉMON SHIELD:
It chomps with its gaping mouth. Its huge jaws are actually steel horns that have been transformed.

Does not evolve.

Meowstic
Constraint Pokémon

Female Form

Male Form

TYPE:
Psychic

How to Say It: MYOW-stik
Imperial Height: 2'
Metric Height: 0.6 m
Imperial Weight: 18.7 lbs.
Metric Weight: 8.5 kg
Gender: ♂ ♀
Ability: Keen Eye / Infiltrator
Weaknesses: Ghost, Dark, Bug

Espurr → Meowstic (male)

→ Meowstic (female)

MALE

POKÉMON SWORD:
Revealing the eyelike patterns on the insides of its ears will unleash its psychic powers. It normally keeps the patterns hidden, however.

POKÉMON SHIELD:
The defensive instinct of the males is strong. It's when they're protecting themselves or their partners that they unleash their full power.

FEMALE

POKÉMON SWORD:
Females are a bit more selfish and aggressive than males. If they don't get what they want, they will torment you with their psychic abilities.

POKÉMON SHIELD:
If it doesn't hold back when it unleashes its psychic power, it can tear apart a tanker. Its unfriendliness is part of its charm.

GALARIAN
Meowth
Scratch Cat Pokémon

TYPE:
Steel

How to Say It: mee-OWTH
Imperial Height: 1'4"
Metric Height: 0.4 m
Imperial Weight: 16.5 lbs.
Metric Weight: 7.5 kg
Gender: ♂ ♀
Ability: Pickup / Tough Claws
Weaknesses: Fire, Fighting, Ground

POKÉMON SWORD:
Living with a savage, seafaring people has toughened this Pokémon's body so much that parts of it have turned to iron.

POKÉMON SHIELD:
These daring Pokémon have coins on their foreheads. Darker coins are harder, and harder coins garner more respect among Meowth.

Galarian Meowth → Perrserker

Meowth

Scratch Cat Pokémon

TYPE:
Normal

How to Say It: mee-OWTH
Imperial Height: 1'4"
Metric Height: 0.4 m
Imperial Weight: 9.3 lbs.
Metric Weight: 4.2 kg
Gender: ♂ ♀
Ability: Pickup / Technician
Weaknesses: Fighting

POKÉMON SWORD:
It loves to collect shiny things. If it's in a good mood, it might even let its Trainer have a look at its hoard of treasures.

POKÉMON SHIELD:
It washes its face regularly to keep the coin on its forehead spotless. It doesn't get along with Galarian Meowth.

Meowth ⇨ Persian

Gigantamax Meowth

Imperial Height: 108'3"+
Metric Height: 33.0+ m
Imperial Weight: ?????.? lbs.
Metric Weight: ?????.? kg

POKÉMON SWORD:
The pattern that has appeared on its giant coin is thought to be the key to unlocking the secrets of the Dynamax phenomenon.

POKÉMON SHIELD:
Its body has grown incredibly long and the coin on its forehead has grown incredibly large—all thanks to Gigantamax power.

Metapod
Cocoon Pokémon

How to Say It: MET-uh-pod
Imperial Height: 2'4"
Metric Height: 0.7 m
Imperial Weight: 21.8 lbs.
Metric Weight: 9.9 kg
Gender: ♂ ♀
Ability: Shed Skin
Weaknesses: Fire, Flying, Rock

POKÉMON SWORD:
It is waiting for the moment to evolve. At this stage, it can only harden, so it remains motionless to avoid attack.

POKÉMON SHIELD:
Even though it is encased in a sturdy shell, the body inside is tender. It can't withstand a harsh attack.

Caterpie ⇨ Metapod ⇨ Butterfree

Milcery
Cream Pokémon

TYPE: Fairy

How to Say It: MIHL-suh-ree
Imperial Height: 8"
Metric Height: 0.2 m
Imperial Weight: 0.7 lbs.
Metric Weight: 0.3 kg
Gender: ♀
Ability: Sweet Veil
Weaknesses: Steel, Poison

POKÉMON SWORD:
This Pokémon was born from sweet-smelling particles in the air. Its body is made of cream.

POKÉMON SHIELD:
They say that any patisserie visited by Milcery is guaranteed success and good fortune.

Milcery ⇨ Alcremie

Milotic

Tender Pokémon

TYPE:
Water

How to Say It: MY-low-tic
Imperial Height: 20'4"
Metric Height: 6.2 m
Imperial Weight: 357.1 lbs.
Metric Weight: 162.0 kg
Gender: ♂ ♀
Ability: Marvel Scale / Competitive
Weaknesses: Electric, Grass

POKÉMON SWORD:
Milotic has provided inspiration to many artists. It has even been referred to as the most beautiful Pokémon of all.

POKÉMON SHIELD:
It's said that a glimpse of a Milotic and its beauty will calm any hostile emotions you're feeling.

Feebas ⇨ **Milotic**

TYPE:
Psychic-
Fairy

Mime Jr.

Mime Pokémon

How to Say It: mime JOO-nyur
Imperial Height: 2'
Metric Height: 0.6 m
Imperial Weight: 28.7 lbs.
Metric Weight: 13.0 kg
Gender: ♂ ♀
Ability: Soundproof / Filter
Weaknesses: Ghost, Steel, Poison

POKÉMON SWORD:
It mimics everyone it sees, but it puts extra effort into copying the graceful dance steps of Mr. Rime as practice.

POKÉMON SHIELD:
It looks for a Mr. Rime that's a good dancer and carefully copies the Mr. Rime's steps like an apprentice.

Mime Jr. ⇨ **Galarian Mr. Mime** ⇨ **Mr. Rime**

Mimikyu
Disguise Pokémon

How to Say It: MEE-mee-kyoo
Imperial Height: 8"
Metric Height: 0.2 m
Imperial Weight: 1.5 lbs.
Metric Weight: 0.7 kg
Gender: ♂ ♀
Ability: Disguise
Weaknesses: Ghost, Steel

POKÉMON SWORD:
It wears a rag fashioned into a Pikachu costume in an effort to look less scary. Unfortunately, the costume only makes it creepier.

POKÉMON SHIELD:
There was a scientist who peeked under Mimikyu's old rag in the name of research. The scientist died of a mysterious disease.

Does not evolve.

TYPE:
Normal

Minccino
Chinchilla Pokémon

How to Say It: min-CHEE-noh
Imperial Height: 1'4"
Metric Height: 0.4 m
Imperial Weight: 12.8 lbs.
Metric Weight: 5.8 kg
Gender: ♂ ♀
Ability: Cute Charm / Technician
Weaknesses: Fighting

POKÉMON SWORD:
The way it brushes away grime with its tail can be helpful when cleaning. But its focus on spotlessness can make cleaning more of a hassle.

POKÉMON SHIELD:
They pet each other with their tails as a form of greeting. Of the two, the one whose tail is fluffier is a bit more boastful.

Minccino ⇨ **Cinccino**

Morelull

Illuminating Pokémon

How to Say It: MORE-eh-lull
Imperial Height: 8"
Metric Height: 0.2 m
Imperial Weight: 3.3 lbs.
Metric Weight: 1.5 kg
Gender: ♂ ♀
Ability: Illuminate / Effect Spore
Weaknesses: Steel, Fire, Flying, Ice, Poison

POKÉMON SWORD:
Pokémon living in the forest eat the delicious caps on Morelull's head. The caps regrow overnight.

POKÉMON SHIELD:
Morelull live in forests that stay dark even during the day. They scatter flickering spores that put enemies to sleep.

Morelull ⇨ **Shiinotic**

Morgrem

Devious Pokémon

How to Say It: MOHR-grehm
Imperial Height: 2'7"
Metric Height: 0.8 m
Imperial Weight: 27.6 lbs.
Metric Weight: 12.5 kg
Gender: ♂
Ability: Prankster / Frisk
Weaknesses: Steel, Fairy, Poison

POKÉMON SWORD:
When it gets down on all fours as if to beg for forgiveness, it's trying to lure opponents in so that it can stab them with its spear-like hair.

POKÉMON SHIELD:
With sly cunning, it tries to lure people into the woods. Some believe it to have the power to make crops grow.

Impidimp Morgrem Grimmsnarl

Morpeko
Two-Sided Pokémon

How to Say It: mohr-PEH-koh
Imperial Height: 1'
Metric Height: 0.3 m
Imperial Weight: 6.6 lbs.
Metric Weight: 3.0 kg
Gender: ♂ ♀
Ability: Hunger Switch
Weaknesses: Fairy, Bug, Fighting, Ground

POKÉMON SWORD:
As it eats the seeds stored up in its pocket-like pouches, this Pokémon is not just satisfying its constant hunger. It's also generating electricity.

POKÉMON SHIELD:
It carries electrically roasted seeds with it as if they're precious treasures. No matter how much it eats, it always gets hungry again in short order.

Does not evolve

GALARIAN
Mr. Mime
Dancing Pokémon

TYPE:
Ice-
Psychic

How to Say It: MIS-ter-MIME
Imperial Height: 4'7"
Metric Height: 1.4 m
Imperial Weight: 125.2 lbs.
Metric Weight: 56.8 kg
Gender: ♂ ♀
Ability: Vital Spirit / Screen Cleaner
Weaknesses: Steel, Ghost, Fire, Dark, Rock, Bug

POKÉMON SWORD:
Its talent is tap-dancing. It can also manipulate temperatures to create a floor of ice, which this Pokémon can kick up to use as a barrier.

POKÉMON SHIELD:
It can radiate chilliness from the bottoms of its feet. It'll spend the whole day tap-dancing on a frozen floor.

Mime Jr. ⇒ **Galarian Mr. Mime** ⇒ **Mr. Rime**

Mr. Rime

Comedian Pokémon

TYPE:
Ice-
Psychic

How to Say It: MIS-ter RYME
Imperial Height: 4'11"
Metric Height: 1.5 m
Imperial Weight: 128.3 lbs.
Metric Weight: 58.2 kg
Gender: ♂ ♀
Ability: Tangled Feet / Screen Cleaner
Weaknesses: Ice Psychic

POKÉMON SWORD:
It's highly skilled at tap-dancing. It waves its cane of ice in time with its graceful movements.

POKÉMON SHIELD:
Its amusing movements make it very popular. It releases its psychic power from the pattern on its belly.

Mime Jr. ⇒ Galarian Mr. Mime ⇒ Mr. Rime

Mudbray

Donkey Pokémon

TYPE:
Ground

How to Say It: MUD-bray
Imperial Height: 3'3"
Metric Height: 1.0 m
Imperial Weight: 242.5 lbs.
Metric Weight: 110.0 kg
Gender: ♂ ♀
Ability: Own Tempo / Stamina
Weaknesses: Water, Grass, Ice

POKÉMON SWORD:
Loads weighing up to 50 times as much as its own body weight pose no issue for this Pokémon. It's skilled at making use of mud.

POKÉMON SHIELD:
It eats dirt to create mud and smears this mud all over its feet, giving them the grip needed to walk on rough terrain without slipping.

 ⇒

Mudbray   Mudsdale

Mudsdale

Draft Horse Pokémon

How to Say It: MUDZ-dale
Imperial Height: 8'2"
Metric Height: 2.5 m
Imperial Weight: 2028.3 lbs.
Metric Weight: 920.0 kg
Gender: ♂ ♀
Ability: Own Tempo / Stamina
Weaknesses: Water, Grass, Ice

POKÉMON SWORD:
Mud that hardens around a Mudsdale's legs sets harder than stone. It's so hard that it allows this Pokémon to scrap a truck with a single kick.

POKÉMON SHIELD:
Mudsdale has so much stamina that it could carry over 10 tons across the Galar region without rest or sleep.

Mudbray ➡ **Mudsdale**

Munchlax

Big Eater Pokémon

TYPE: Normal

How to Say It: MUNCH-lax
Imperial Height: 2'
Metric Height: 0.6 m
Imperial Weight: 231.5 lbs.
Metric Weight: 105.0 kg
Gender: ♂ ♀
Ability: Pickup / Thick Fat
Weaknesses: Fighting

POKÉMON SWORD:
Stuffing itself with vast amounts of food is its only concern. Whether the food is rotten or fresh, yummy or tasteless—it does not care.

POKÉMON SHIELD:
It stores food beneath its fur. It might share just one bite, but only if it really trusts you.

Munchlax ➡ **Snorlax**

Munna
Dream Eater Pokémon

TYPE:
Psychic

How to Say It: MOON-nuh
Imperial Height: 2'
Metric Height: 0.6 m
Imperial Weight: 51.4 lbs.
Metric Weight: 23.3 kg
Gender: ♂ ♀
Ability: Forewarn / Synchronize
Weaknesses: Bug, Ghost, Dark

POKÉMON SWORD:
Late at night, it appears beside people's pillows. As it feeds on dreams, the patterns on its body give off a faint glow.

POKÉMON SHIELD:
It eats dreams and releases mist. The mist is pink when it's eating a good dream, and black when it's eating a nightmare.

Munna   Musharna

TYPE:
Psychic

Musharna
Drowsing Pokémon

How to Say It: moo-SHAHR-nuh
Imperial Height: 3'7"
Metric Height: 1.1 m
Imperial Weight: 133.4 lbs.
Metric Weight: 60.5 kg
Gender: ♂ ♀
Ability: Forewarn / Synchronize
Weaknesses: Bug, Ghost, Dark

POKÉMON SWORD:
When dark mists emanate from its body, don't get too near. If you do, your nightmares will become reality.

POKÉMON SHIELD:
It drowses and dreams all the time. It's best to leave it be if it's just woken up, as it's a terrible grump when freshly roused from sleep.

Munna   Musharna

Natu
Tiny Bird Pokémon

TYPE:
Psychic-
Flying

How to Say It: NAH-too
Imperial Height: 8"
Metric Height: 0.2 m
Imperial Weight: 4.4 lbs.
Metric Weight: 2.0 kg
Gender: ♂ ♀
Ability: Synchronize / Early Bird
Weaknesses: Dark, Electric, Ghost, Ice, Rock

POKÉMON SWORD:
It is extremely good at climbing tree trunks and likes to eat the new sprouts on the trees.

POKÉMON SHIELD:
Because its wings aren't yet fully grown, it has to hop to get around. It is always staring at something.

Natu   Xatu

Nickit
Fox Pokémon

TYPE:
Dark

How to Say It: NICK-it
Imperial Height: 2'
Metric Height: 0.6 m
Imperial Weight: 19.6 lbs.
Metric Weight: 8.9 kg
Gender: ♂ ♀
Ability: Run Away / Unburden
Weaknesses: Fairy, Bug, Fighting

POKÉMON SWORD:
Aided by the soft pads on its feet, it silently raids the food stores of other Pokémon. It survives off its ill-gotten gains.

POKÉMON SHIELD:
Cunning and cautious, this Pokémon survives by stealing food from others. It erases its tracks with swipes of its tail as it makes off with its plunder.

Nickit   Thievul

Nincada

Trainee Pokémon

TYPE:
Bug-Ground

How to Say It: nin-KAH-da
Imperial Height: 1'8"
Metric Height: 0.5 m
Imperial Weight: 12.1 lbs.
Metric Weight: 5.5 kg
Gender: ♂ ♀
Ability: Compound Eyes
Weaknesses: Fire, Flying, Ice, Water

POKÉMON SWORD:
Because it lived almost entirely underground, it is nearly blind. It uses its antennae instead.

POKÉMON SHIELD:
It can sometimes live underground for more than 10 years. It absorbs nutrients from the roots of trees.

Ninjask

Nincada

Shedinja

Ninetales

TYPE:
Fire

Fox Pokémon

How to Say It: NINE-tails
Imperial Height: 3'7"
Metric Height: 1.1 m
Imperial Weight: 43.9 lbs.
Metric Weight: 19.9 kg
Gender: ♂ ♀
Ability: Flash Fire
Weaknesses: Ground, Rock, Water

POKÉMON SWORD:
It is said to live 1,000 years, and each of its tails is loaded with supernatural powers.

POKÉMON SHIELD:
Very smart and very vengeful. Grabbing one of its many tails could result in a 1,000-year curse.

Vulpix

Ninetales

Ninjask
Ninja Pokémon

How to Say It: NIN-jask
Imperial Height: 2'7"
Metric Height: 0.8 m
Imperial Weight: 26.5 lbs.
Metric Weight: 12.0 kg
Gender: ♂♀
Ability: Speed Boost
Weaknesses: Rock, Electric, Fire, Flying, Ice

POKÉMON SWORD:
Its cry leaves a lasting headache if heard for too long. It moves so quickly that it is almost invisible.

POKÉMON SHIELD:
This Pokémon is so quick, it is said to be able to avoid any attack. It loves to feed on tree sap.

Ninjask

Nincada

Shedinja

Noctowl
Owl Pokémon

How to Say It: NAHK-towl
Imperial Height: 5'3"
Metric Height: 1.6 m
Imperial Weight: 89.9 lbs.
Metric Weight: 40.8 kg
Gender: ♂♀
Ability: Insomnia / Keen Eye
Weaknesses: Electric, Ice, Rock

POKÉMON SWORD:
Its eyes are specially developed to enable it to see clearly even in murky darkness and minimal light.

POKÉMON SHIELD:
When it needs to think, it rotates its head 180 degrees to sharpen its intellectual power.

Hoothoot

Noctowl

Noibat

Sound Wave Pokémon

TYPE:
Flying-
Dragon

How to Say It: NOY-bat
Imperial Height: 1'8"
Metric Height: 0.5 m
Imperial Weight: 17.6 lbs.
Metric Weight: 8.0 kg
Gender: ♂ ♀
Ability: Frisk / Infiltrator
Weaknesses: Ice, Rock, Fairy, Dragon

POKÉMON SWORD:
After nightfall, they emerge from the caves they nest in during the day. Using their ultrasonic waves, they go on the hunt for ripened fruit.

POKÉMON SHIELD:
No wavelength of sound is beyond Noibat's ability to produce. The ultrasonic waves it generates can overcome much larger Pokémon.

Noibat ⇨ Noivern

TYPE:
Flying-
Dragon

Noivern

Sound Wave Pokémon

How to Say It: NOY-vurn
Imperial Height: 4'11"
Metric Height: 1.5 m
Imperial Weight: 187.4 lbs.
Metric Weight: 85.0 kg
Gender: ♂ ♀
Ability: Frisk / Infiltrator
Weaknesses: Fairy, Dragon, Ice, Rock

POKÉMON SWORD:
Aggressive and cruel, this Pokémon will ruthlessly torment enemies that are helpless in the dark.

POKÉMON SHIELD:
Flying through the darkness, it weakens enemies with ultrasonic waves that could crush stone. Its fangs finish the fight.

Noibat ⇨ Noivern

Nuzleaf
Wily Pokémon

TYPE:
Grass-Dark

How to Say It: NUHZ-leef
Imperial Height: 3'3"
Metric Height: 1.0 m
Imperial Weight: 61.7 lbs.
Metric Weight: 28.0 kg
Gender: ♂ ♀
Ability: Chlorophyll / Early Bird
Weaknesses: Bug, Fire, Fighting, Flying, Ice, Poison, Fairy

POKÉMON SWORD:
It lives deep in forests. With the leaf on its head, it makes a flute whose song makes listeners uneasy.

POKÉMON SHIELD:
They live in holes bored in large trees. The sound of Nuzleaf's grass flute fills listeners with dread.

Seedot   Nuzleaf   Shiftry

Obstagoon
Blocking Pokémon

TYPE:
Dark-Normal

How to Say It: AHB-stuh-goon
Imperial Height: 5'3"
Metric Height: 1.6 m
Imperial Weight: 101.4 lbs.
Metric Weight: 46.0 kg
Gender: ♂ ♀
Ability: Reckless / Guts
Weaknesses: Fairy, Bug, Fighting

POKÉMON SWORD:
Its voice is staggering in volume. Obstagoon has a tendency to take on a threatening posture and shout—this move is known as Obstruct.

POKÉMON SHIELD:
It evolved after experiencing numerous fights. While crossing its arms, it lets out a shout that would make any opponent flinch.

Galarian Zigzagoon   Galarian Linoone   Obstagoon

Octillery
Jet Pokémon

TYPE:
Water

How to Say It: ock-TILL-er-ree
Imperial Height: 2'11"
Metric Height: 0.9 m
Imperial Weight: 62.8 lbs.
Metric Weight: 28.5 kg
Gender: ♂♀
Ability: Suction Cups / Sniper
Weaknesses: Electric, Grass

POKÉMON SWORD:
It has a tendency to want to be in holes. It prefers rock crags or pots and sprays ink from them before attacking.

POKÉMON SHIELD:
It traps enemies with its suction-cupped tentacles, then smashes them with its rock-hard head.

Remoraid   Octillery

TYPE:
Grass-Poison

Oddish
Weed Pokémon

How to Say It: ODD-ish
Imperial Height: 1'8"
Metric Height: 0.5 m
Imperial Weight: 11.9 lbs.
Metric Weight: 5.4 kg
Gender: ♂♀
Ability: Chlorophyll
Weaknesses: Fire, Flying, Ice, Psychic

POKÉMON SWORD:
If exposed to moonlight, it starts to move. It roams far and wide at night to scatter its seeds.

POKÉMON SHIELD:
During the day, it stays in the cold underground to avoid the sun. It grows by bathing in moonlight.

Vileplume

Oddish   Gloom

Bellossom

157

Onix
Rock Snake Pokémon

How to Say It: ON-icks
Imperial Height: 28'10"
Metric Height: 8.8 m
Imperial Weight: 463.0 lbs.
Metric Weight: 210.0 kg
Gender: ♂ ♀
Ability: Rock Head / Sturdy
Weaknesses: Grass, Water, Fighting, Ground, Ice, Steel

POKÉMON SWORD:
As it digs through the ground, it absorbs many hard objects. This is what makes its body so solid.

POKÉMON SHIELD:
It rapidly bores through the ground at 50 mph by squirming and twisting its massive, rugged body.

Onix ⇨ Steelix

Oranguru
Sage Pokémon

How to Say It: or-RANG-goo-roo
Imperial Height: 4'11'
Metric Height: 1.5 m
Imperial Weight: 167.6 lbs.
Metric Weight: 76.0 kg
Gender: ♂ ♀
Ability: Inner Focus / Telepathy
Weaknesses: Dark, Bug

POKÉMON SWORD:
With waves of its fan—made from leaves and its own fur—Oranguru skillfully gives instructions to other Pokémon.

POKÉMON SHIELD:
It knows the forest inside and out. If it comes across a wounded Pokémon, Oranguru will gather medicinal herbs to treat it.

Does not evolve.

Orbeetle
Seven Spot Pokémon

TYPE:
Bug-
Psychic

How to Say It: OR-BEE-del
Imperial Height: 1'4"
Metric Height: 0.4 m
Imperial Weight: 89.9 lbs.
Metric Weight: 40.8 kg
Gender: ♂ ♀
Ability: Swarm / Frisk
Weaknesses: Ghost, Fire, Flying,
Dark, Rock, Bug

POKÉMON SWORD:
It's famous for its high level of intelligence, and the large size of its brain is proof that it also possesses immense psychic power.

POKÉMON SHIELD:
It emits psychic energy to observe and study what's around it—and what's around it can include things over six miles away.

Blipbug　　**Dottler**　　**Orbeetle**

Gigantamax Orbeetle

POKÉMON SWORD:
Its brain has grown to a gargantuan size, as has the rest of its body. This Pokémon's intellect and psychic abilities are overpowering.

POKÉMON SHIELD:
If it were to utilize every last bit of its power, it could control the minds of every living being in its vicinity.

Imperial Height: 45'11"
Metric Height: 14.0 m
Imperial Weight: ?????.? lbs.
Metric Weight: ?????.? kg

159

Palpitoad
Vibration Pokémon

How to Say It: PAL-pih-tohd
Imperial Height: 2'7"
Metric Height: 0.8 m
Imperial Weight: 37.5 lbs.
Metric Weight: 17.0 kg
Gender: ♂♀
Ability: Soft Swim / Hydration
Weaknesses: Grass

POKÉMON SWORD:
It weakens its prey with sound waves intense enough to cause headaches, then entangles them with its sticky tongue.

POKÉMON SHIELD:
On occasion, their cries are sublimely pleasing to the ear. Palpitoad with larger lumps on their bodies can sing with a wider range of sounds.

Tympole   Palpitoad   Seismitoad

TYPE:
Fighting

Pancham
Playful Pokémon

How to Say It: PAN-chum
Imperial Height: 2'
Metric Height: 0.6 m
Imperial Weight: 17.6 lbs.
Metric Weight: 8.0 kg
Gender: ♂♀
Ability: Iron Fist / Mold Breaker
Weaknesses: Psychic, Flying, Fairy

POKÉMON SWORD:
It chooses a Pangoro as its master and then imitates its master's actions. This is how it learns to battle and hunt for prey.

POKÉMON SHIELD:
Wanting to make sure it's taken seriously, Pancham's always giving others a glare. But if it's not focusing, it ends up smiling.

Pancham   Pangoro

Pangoro
Daunting Pokémon

How to Say It: PAN-go-roh
Imperial Height: 6'11"
Metric Height: 2.1 m
Imperial Weight: 299.8 lbs.
Metric Weight: 136.0 kg
Gender: ♂♀
Ability: Iron Fist / Mold Breaker
Weaknesses: Flying, Fairy, Fighting

POKÉMON SWORD:
This Pokémon is quick to anger, and it has no problem using its prodigious strength to get its way. It lives for duels against Obstagoon.

POKÉMON SHIELD:
Using its leaf, Pangoro can predict the moves of its opponents. It strikes with punches that can turn a dump truck into scrap with just one hit.

Pancham   Pangoro

Passimian
Teamwork Pokémon

TYPE:
Fighting

How to Say It: pass-SIM-ee-uhn
Imperial Height: 6'7"
Metric Height: 2.0 m
Imperial Weight: 182.5 lbs.
Metric Weight: 82.8 kg
Gender: ♂♀
Ability: Receiver
Weaknesses: Psychic, Flying, Fairy

POKÉMON SWORD:
Displaying amazing teamwork, they follow the orders of their boss as they all help out in the search for their favorite berries.

POKÉMON SHIELD:
Passimian live in groups of about 20, with each member performing an assigned role. Through cooperation, the group survives.

Does not evolve.

Pawniard
Sharp Blade Pokémon

TYPE:
Dark-Steel

How to Say It: PAWN-yard
Imperial Height: 1'8"
Metric Height: 0.5 m
Imperial Weight: 22.5 lbs.
Metric Weight: 10.2 kg
Gender: ♂ ♀
Ability: Defiant / Inner Focus
Weaknesses: Fighting, Fire, Ground

POKÉMON SWORD:
It uses river stones to maintain the cutting edges of the blades covering its body. These sharpened blades allow it to bring down opponents.

POKÉMON SHIELD:
A pack of these Pokémon forms to serve a Bisharp boss. Each Pawniard trains diligently, dreaming of one day taking the lead.

Pawniard ⇨ Bisharp

TYPE:
Water-Flyring

Pelipper
Water Bird Pokémon

How to Say It: PEL-ip-purr
Imperial Height: 3'11"
Metric Height: 1.2 m
Imperial Weight: 61.7 lbs.
Metric Weight: 28.0 kg
Gender: ♂ ♀
Ability: Keen Eye / Drizzle
Weaknesses: Electric, Rock

POKÉMON SWORD:
It is a messenger of the skies, carrying small Pokémon and eggs to safety in its bill.

POKÉMON SHIELD:
Skimming the water's surface, it dips its large bill in the sea, scoops up food and water, and carries it.

Wingull ⇨ Pelipper

Perrserker
Viking Pokémon

How to Say It: purr-ZURR-kurr
Imperial Height: 2'7"
Metric Height: 0.8 m
Imperial Weight: 61.7 lbs.
Metric Weight: 28.0 kg
Gender: ♂ ♀
Ability: Battle Armor / Tough Claws
Weaknesses: Fire, Fighting, Ground

POKÉMON SWORD:
What appears to be an iron helmet is actually hardened hair. This Pokémon lives for the thrill of battle.

POKÉMON SHIELD:
After many battles, it evolved dangerous claws that come together to form daggers when extended.

Galarian Meowth ⇨ Perrserker

Persian
Classy Cat Pokémon

TYPE:
Normal

How to Say It: PER-zhun
Imperial Height: 3'3"
Metric Height: 1.0 m
Imperial Weight: 70.5 lbs.
Metric Weight: 32.0 kg
Gender: ♂ ♀
Ability: Limber / Technician
Weaknesses: Fighting

POKÉMON SWORD:
Getting this prideful Pokémon to warm up to you takes a lot of effort, and it will claw at you the moment it gets annoyed.

POKÉMON SHIELD:
Its elegant and refined behavior clashes with that of the barbaric Perrserker. The relationship between the two is one of mutual disdain.

Meowth ⇨ Persian

TYPE:
Ghost-
Grass

Phantump
Stump Pokémon

How to Say It: FAN-tump
Imperial Height: 1'4"
Metric Height: 0.4 m
Imperial Weight: 15.4 lbs.
Metric Weight: 7.0 kg
Gender: ♂ ♀
Ability: Natural Cure / Frisk
Weaknesses: Ghost, Fire, Flying, Dark, Ice

POKÉMON SWORD:
After a lost child perished in the forest, their spirit possessed a tree stump, causing the spirit's rebirth as this Pokémon.

POKÉMON SHIELD:
With a voice like a human child's, it cries out to lure adults deep into the forest, getting them lost among the trees.

Phantump ⇨ Trevenant

Pichu

Tiny Mouse Pokémon

TYPE:
Electric

How to Say It: PEE-choo
Imperial Height: 1'
Metric Height: 0.3 m
Imperial Weight: 4.4 lbs.
Metric Weight: 2.0 kg
Gender: ♂♀
Ability: Static
Weaknesses: Ground

POKÉMON SWORD:
Despite its small size, it can zap even adult humans. However, if it does so, it also surprises itself.

POKÉMON SHIELD:
The electric sacs in its cheeks are small. If even a little electricity leaks, it becomes shocked.

Pichu   Pikachu   Raichu

Pidove

Tiny Pigeon Pokémon

TYPE:
Normal-
Flying

How to Say It: pih-DUV
Imperial Height: 1'
Metric Height: 0.3 m
Imperial Weight: 4.6 lbs.
Metric Weight: 2.1 kg
Gender: ♂♀
Ability: Bick Pecks / Super Luck
Weaknesses: Electric, Ice, Rock

POKÉMON SWORD:
Where people go, these Pokémon follow. If you're scattering food for them, be careful— several hundred of them can gather at once.

POKÉMON SHIELD:
It's forgetful and not very bright, but many Trainers love it anyway for its friendliness and sincerity.

Pidove   Tranquill   Unfezant (male)

Unfezant (female)

Pikachu
Mouse Pokémon

TYPE:
Electric

How to Say It: PEE-ka-choo
Imperial Height: 1'4"
Metric Height: 0.4 m
Imperial Weight: 13.2 lbs.
Metric Weight: 6.0 kg
Gender: ♂ ♀
Ability: Static
Weaknesses: Ground

POKÉMON SWORD:
Pikachu that can generate powerful electricity have cheek sacs that are extra soft and super stretchy.

POKÉMON SHIELD:
When Pikachu meet, they'll touch their tails together and exchange electricity through them as a form of greeting.

Pichu

Pikachu

Raichu

Gigantamax Pikachu

Imperial Height: 68'11"+
Metric Height: 21.0+ m
Imperial Weight: ?????.? lbs.
Metric Weight: ?????.? kg

POKÉMON SWORD:
Its Gigantamax power expanded, forming its supersized body and towering tail.

POKÉMON SHIELD:
When it smashes its opponents with its bolt- shaped tail, it delivers a surge of electricity equivalent to a lightning strike.

Piloswine
Swine Pokémon

How to Say It: PILE-oh-swine
Imperial Height: 3'7"
Metric Height: 1.1 m
Imperial Weight: 123.0 lbs.
Metric Weight: 55.8 kg
Gender: ♂ ♀
Ability: Oblivious / Snow Cloak
Weaknesses: Fighting, Fire,
  Grass, Steel, Water

POKÉMON SWORD:
If it charges at an enemy, the hairs on its back stand up straight. It is very sensitive to sound.

POKÉMON SHIELD:
Although its legs are short, its rugged hooves prevent it from slipping, even on icy ground.

Swinub ➡ Piloswine ➡ Mamoswine

TYPE:
Electric

Pincurchin
Sea Urchin Pokémon

How to Say It: PIN-kur-chin
Imperial Height: 1'
Metric Height: 0.3 m
Imperial Weight: 2.2 lbs.
Metric Weight: 1.0 kg
Gender: ♂ ♀
Ability: Lightning Rod
Weaknesses: Ground

POKÉMON SWORD:
It feeds on seaweed, using its teeth to scrape it off rocks. Electric current flows from the tips of its spines.

POKÉMON SHIELD:
It stores electricity in each spine. Even if one gets broken off, it still continues to emit electricity for at least three hours.

Does not evolve.

Polteageist
Black Tea Pokémon

TYPE:
Ghost

How to Say It: POHL-tee-guyst
Imperial Height: 8"
Metric Height: 0.2 m
Imperial Weight: 0.9 lbs.
Metric Weight: 0.4 kg
Gender: ♂♀
Ability: Weak Armor
Weaknesses: Ghost, Dark

POKÉMON SWORD:
This species lives in antique teapots. Most pots are forgeries, but on rare occasions, an authentic work is found.

POKÉMON SHIELD:
Leaving leftover black tea unattended is asking for this Pokémon to come along and pour itself into it, turning the tea into a new Polteageist.

Sinistea **Polteageist**

GALARIAN
Ponyta
Unique Horse Pokémon

TYPE:
Psychic

How to Say It: POH-nee-tah
Imperial Height: 2'7"
Metric Height: 0.8 m
Imperial Weight: 52.9 lbs.
Metric Weight: 24.0 kg
Gender: ♂♀
Ability: Run Away / Pastel Veil
Weaknesses: Ghost, Dark, Bug

POKÉMON SWORD:
Its small horn hides a healing power. With a few rubs from this Pokémon's horn, any slight wound you have will be healed.

POKÉMON SHIELD:
This Pokémon will look into your eyes and read the contents of your heart. If it finds evil there, it promptly hides away.

Galarian Ponyta **Galarian Rapidash**

Pumpkaboo
Pumpkin Pokémon

How to Say It: PUMP-kuh-boo
Imperial Height: 1'4"
Metric Height: 0.4 m
Imperial Weight: 11.0 lbs.
Metric Weight: 5.0 kg
Gender: ♂ ♀
Ability: Pickup / Frisk
Weaknesses: Ghost, Fire, Flying,
Dark, Ice

POKÉMON SWORD:
Spirits that wander this world are placed into Pumpkaboo's body. They're then moved on to the afterlife.

POKÉMON SHIELD:
The light that streams out from the holes in the pumpkin can hypnotize and control the people and Pokémon that see it.

Pumpkaboo   Gourgeist

TYPE:
Rock-
Ground

Pupitar
Hard Shell Pokémon

How to Say It: PUE-puh-tar
Imperial Height: 3'11"
Metric Height: 1.2 m
Imperial Weight: 335.1 lbs.
Metric Weight: 152.0 kg
Gender: ♂ ♀
Ability: Shed Skin
Weaknesses: Grass, Water, Fighting,
Ground, Ice, Steel

POKÉMON SWORD:
Even sealed in its shell, it can move freely. Hard and fast, it has outstanding destructive power.

POKÉMON SHIELD:
It will not stay still, even while it's a pupa. It already has arms and legs under its solid shell.

Larvitar   Pupitar   Tyranitar

Purrloin

Devious Pokémon

How to Say It: PUR-loyn
Imperial Height: 1'4"
Metric Height: 0.4 m
Imperial Weight: 22.3 lbs.
Metric Weight: 10.1 kg
Gender: ♂ ♀
Ability: Limber / Unburden
Weaknesses: Fighting, Bug, Fairy

POKÉMON SWORD:
It steals things from people just to amuse itself with their frustration. A rivalry exists between this Pokémon and Nickit.

POKÉMON SHIELD:
Opponents that get drawn in by its adorable behavior come away with stinging scratches from its claws and stinging pride from its laughter.

Purrloin ⇨ Liepard

Pyukumuku

Sea Cucumber Pokémon

TYPE: Water

How to Say It: PYOO-koo-MOO-koo
Imperial Height: 1'
Metric Height: 0.3 m
Imperial Weight: 2.6 lbs.
Metric Weight: 1.2 kg
Gender: ♂ ♀
Ability: Innards Out
Weaknesses: Grass, Electric

POKÉMON SWORD:
It lives in warm, shallow waters. If it encounters a foe, it will spit out its internal organs as a means to punch them.

POKÉMON SHIELD:
It's covered in a slime that keeps its skin moist, allowing it to stay on land for days without drying up.

Does not evolve.

Quagsire
Water Fish Pokémon

TYPE:
Water-Ground

How to Say It: KWAG-sire
Imperial Height: 4'7"
Metric Height: 1.4 m
Imperial Weight: 165.3 lbs.
Metric Weight: 75.0 kg
Gender: ♂ ♀
Ability: Damp, Water Absorb
Weaknesses: Grass

POKÉMON SWORD:
It has an easygoing nature. It doesn't care if it bumps its head on boats and boulders while swimming.

POKÉMON SHIELD:
Its body is always slimy. It often bangs its head on the river bottom as it swims but seems not to care.

Wooper ⇨ Quagsire

TYPE:
Water-Poison

Qwilfish
Balloon Pokémon

How to Say It: KWIL-fish
Imperial Height: 1'8"
Metric Height: 0.5 m
Imperial Weight: 8.6 lbs.
Metric Weight: 3.9 kg
Gender: ♂ ♀
Ability: Poison Point / Swift Swim
Weaknesses: Electric, Ground, Psychic

POKÉMON SWORD:
When faced with a larger opponent, it swallows as much water as it can to match the opponent's size.

POKÉMON SHIELD:
The small spikes covering its body developed from scales. They inject a toxin that causes fainting.

Does not evolve.

Raboot
Rabbit Pokémon

TYPE:
Fire

How to Say It: RAB-boot
Imperial Height: 2'
Metric Height: 0.6 m
Imperial Weight: 19.8 lbs.
Metric Weight: 9.0 kg
Gender: ♂ ♀
Ability: Blaze
Weaknesses: Water, Ground, Rock

POKÉMON SWORD:
Its thick and fluffy fur protects it from the cold and enables it to use hotter fire moves.

POKÉMON SHIELD:
It kicks berries right off the branches of trees and then juggles them with its feet, practicing its footwork.

Scorbunny   Raboot   Cinderac

TYPE:
Electric

Raichu
Mouse Pokémon

How to Say It: RYE-choo
Imperial Height: 2'7"
Metric Height: 0.8 m
Imperial Weight: 66.1 lbs.
Metric Weight: 30.0 kg
Gender: ♂ ♀
Ability: Static
Weaknesses: Ground

POKÉMON SWORD:
Its long tail serves as a ground to protect itself from its own high-voltage power.

POKÉMON SHIELD:
If its electric pouches run empty, it raises its tail to gather electricity from the atmosphere.

Pichu   Pikachu   Raichu

Ralts
Feeling Pokémon

TYPE:
Psychic-
Fairy

How to Say It: RALTS
Imperial Height: 1'4"
Metric Height: 0.4 m
Imperial Weight: 14.6 lbs.
Metric Weight: 6.6 kg
Gender: ♂ ♀
Ability: Synchronize / Trace
Weaknesses: Ghost, Steel, Poison

POKÉMON SWORD:
It is highly attuned to the emotions of people and Pokémon. It hides if it senses hostility.

POKÉMON SHIELD:
If its horns capture the warm feelings of people or Pokémon, its body warms up slightly.

Ralts   Kirlia   Gardevoir

Gallade

GALARIAN
Rapidash
Unique Horn Pokémon

TYPE:
Psychic-
Fairy

How to Say It: RAP-id-dash
Imperial Height: 5'7"
Metric Height: 1.7 m
Imperial Weight: 176.4 lbs.
Metric Weight: 80.0 kg
Gender: ♂ ♀
Ability: Run Away / Pastel Veil
Weaknesses: Ghost, Steel, Poison

POKÉMON SWORD:
Little can stand up to its psycho cut. Unleashed from this Pokémon's horn, the move will punch a hole right through a thick metal sheet.

POKÉMON SHIELD:
Brave and prideful, this Pokémon dashes airily through the forest, its steps aided by the psychic power stored in the fur on its fetlocks.

Galarian
Ponyta   Galarian
Rapidash

Remoraid

Jet Pokémon

How to Say It: REM-oh-raid
Imperial Height: 2'
Metric Height: 0.6 m
Imperial Weight: 26.5 lbs.
Metric Weight: 12 kg
Gender: ♂♀
Ability: Hustle / Sniper
Weaknesses: Electric, Grass

POKÉMON SWORD:
The water they shoot from their mouths can hit moving prey from more than 300 feet away.

POKÉMON SHIELD:
Using its dorsal fin as a suction pad, it clings to a Mantine's underside to scavenge for leftovers.

Remoraid **Octillery**

Reuniclus

TYPE: Psychic

Multiplying Pokémon

How to Say It: ree-yoo-NEE-klus
Imperial Height: 3'3"
Metric Height: 1.0 m
Imperial Weight: 44.3 lbs.
Metric Weight: 20.1 kg
Gender: ♂♀
Ability: Overcoat / Magic Guard
Weaknesses: Bug, Ghost, Dark

POKÉMON SWORD:
While it could use its psychic abilities in battle, this Pokémon prefers to swing its powerful arms around to beat opponents into submission.

POKÉMON SHIELD:
It's said that drinking the liquid surrounding Reuniclus grants wisdom. Problem is, the liquid is highly toxic to anything besides Reuniclus itself.

Solosis **Duosion** **Reuniclus**

Rhydon
Drill Pokémon

TYPE: Ground-Rock

How to Say It: RYE-don
Imperial Height: 6'3"
Metric Height: 1.9 m
Imperial Weight: 264.6 lbs.
Metric Weight: 120.0 kg
Gender: ♂ ♀
Ability: Lightning Rod / Rock Head
Weaknesses: Grass, Water, Fighting, Ground, Ice, Steel

POKÉMON SWORD:
It begins walking on its hind legs after evolution. It can punch holes through boulders with its horn.

POKÉMON SHIELD:
Protected by an armor-like hide, it is capable of living in molten lava of 3,600 degrees Fahrenheit.

Rhyhorn   Rhydon   Rhyperior

TYPE: Ground-Rock

Rhyhorn
Spikes Pokémon

How to Say It: RYE-horn
Imperial Height: 3'3"
Metric Height: 1.0 m
Imperial Weight: 253.5 lbs.
Metric Weight: 115.0 kg
Gender: ♂ ♀
Ability: Lightning Rod / Rock Head
Weaknesses: Grass, Water, Fighting, Ground, Ice, Steel

POKÉMON SWORD:
Strong, but not too bright, this Pokémon can shatter even a skyscraper with its charging tackles.

POKÉMON SHIELD:
It can remember only one thing at a time. Once it starts rushing, it forgets why it started.

Rhyhorn   Rhydon   Rhyperior

Rhyperior
Drill Pokémon

TYPE:
Ground-Rock

How to Say It: rye-PEER-ee-or
Imperial Height: 7'10"
Metric Height: 2.4 m
Imperial Weight: 623.5 lbs.
Metric Weight: 282.8 kg
Gender: ♂ ♀
Ability: Lightning Rod / Solid Rock
Weaknesses: Grass, Water, Fighting, Ground, Ice, Steel

POKÉMON SWORD:
It can load up to three projectiles per arm into the holes in its hands. What launches out of those holes could be either rocks or Roggenrola.

POKÉMON SHIELD:
It relies on its carapace to deflect incoming attacks and throw its enemy off balance. As soon as that happens, it drives its drill into the foe.

Rhyhorn ➡ Rhydon ➡ Rhyperior

Ribombee
Bee Fly Pokémon

TYPE:
Bug-Fairy

How to Say It: rih-BOMB-bee
Imperial Height: 8"
Metric Height: 0.2 m
Imperial Weight: 1.1 lbs.
Metric Weight: 0.5 kg
Gender: ♂ ♀
Ability: Honey Gather / Shield Dust
Weaknesses: Fire, Steel, Flying, Poison, Rock

POKÉMON SWORD:
It makes pollen puffs from pollen and nectar. The puffs' effects depend on the type of ingredients and how much of each one is used.

POKÉMON SHIELD:
Ribombee absolutely hate getting wet or rained on. In the cloudy Galar region, they are very seldom seen.

Cutiefly ➡ Ribombee

Rillaboom
Drumming Pokémon

TYPE: Grass

How to Say It: RIL-uh-boom
Imperial Height: 6'11"
Metric Height: 2.1 m
Imperial Weight: 198.4 lbs.
Metric Weight: 90.0 kg
Gender: ♂♀
Ability: Overgrow
Weaknesses: Fire, Flying, Ice, Poison, Bug

POKÉMON SWORD:
By drumming, it taps into the power of its special tree stump. The roots of the stump follow its direction in battle.

POKÉMON SHIELD:
The one with the best drumming techniques becomes the boss of the troop. It has a gentle disposition and values harmony among its group.

Grookey Thwackey Rillaboom

Riolu
Emanation Pokémon

TYPE: Fighting

How to Say It: ree-OH-loo
Imperial Height: 2'4"
Metric Height: 0.7 m
Imperial Weight: 44.5 lbs.
Metric Weight: 20.2 kg
Gender: ♂♀
Ability: Steadfast / Inner Focus
Weaknesses: Flying, Psychic, Fairy

POKÉMON SWORD:
It's exceedingly energetic, with enough stamina to keep running all through the night. Taking it for walks can be a challenging experience.

POKÉMON SHIELD:
It can use waves called auras to gauge how others are feeling. These same waves can also tell this Pokémon about the state of the environment.

Riolu Lucario

Roggenrola
Mantle Pokémon

TYPE:
Rock

How to Say It: rah-gen-ROH-lah
Imperial Height: 1'4"
Metric Height: 0.4 m
Imperial Weight: 39.7 lbs.
Metric Weight: 18.0 kg
Gender: ♂ ♀
Ability: Sturdy / Weak Armor
Weaknesses: Water, Grass, Fighting, Ground, Steel

POKÉMON SWORD:
It's as hard as steel, but apparently a long soak in water will cause it to soften a bit.

POKÉMON SHIELD:
When it detects a noise, it starts to move. The energy core inside it makes this Pokémon slightly warm to the touch.

Roggenrola   Boldore   Gigalith

TYPE:
Rock

Rolycoly
Coal Pokémon

How to Say It: ROH-lee-KOH-lee
Imperial Height: 1'
Metric Height: 0.3 m
Imperial Weight: 26.5 lbs.
Metric Weight: 12.0 kg
Gender: ♂ ♀
Ability: Steam Engine / Heatproof
Weaknesses: Water, Steel, Grass, Fighting, Ground

POKÉMON SWORD:
Most of its body has the same composition as coal. Fittingly, this Pokémon was first discovered in coal mines about 400 years ago.

POKÉMON SHIELD:
It can race around like a unicycle, even on rough, rocky terrain. Burning coal sustains it.

Rolycoly   Carkol   Coalossal

Rookidee
Tiny Bird Pokémon

How to Say It: ROOK-ih-dee
Imperial Height: 8"
Metric Height: 0.2 m
Imperial Weight: 4.0 lbs.
Metric Weight: 1.8 kg
Gender: ♂ ♀
Ability: Keen Eye / Unnerve
Weaknesses: Electric, Ice, Rock

POKÉMON SWORD:
It will bravely challenge any opponent, no matter how powerful. This Pokémon benefits from every battle—even a defeat increases its strength a bit.

POKÉMON SHIELD:
Jumping nimbly about, this small-bodied Pokémon takes advantage of even the slightest opportunity to disorient larger opponents.

Rookidee   Corvisquire   Corviknight

Roselia
Thorn Pokémon

How to Say It: roh-ZEH-lee-uh
Imperial Height: 1'
Metric Height: 0.3 m
Imperial Weight: 4.4 lbs.
Metric Weight: 2.0 kg
Gender: ♂ ♀
Ability: Natural Cure / Poison Point
Weaknesses: Fire, Flying, Ice, Psychic

POKÉMON SWORD:
Its flowers give off a relaxing fragrance. The stronger its aroma, the healthier the Roselia is.

POKÉMON SHIELD:
It uses the different poisons in each hand separately when it attacks. The stronger its aroma, the healthier it is.

Budew   Roselia   Roserade

Roserade
Bouquet Pokémon

TYPE:
Grass-
Poison

How to Say It: ROSE-raid
Imperial Height: 2'11"
Metric Height: 0.9 m
Imperial Weight: 32.0 lbs.
Metric Weight: 14.5 kg
Gender: ♂ ♀
Ability: Natural Cure / Poison Point
Weaknesses: Fire, Flying, Ice, Psychic

POKÉMON SWORD:
After captivating opponents with its sweet scent, it lashes them with its thorny whips.

POKÉMON SHIELD:
The poison in its right hand is quick acting. The poison in its left hand is slow acting. Both are life threatening.

Budew   Roselia   Roserade

Rotom
Plasma Pokémon

Wash Rotom

Heat Rotom

Frost Rotom

Fan Rotom

Mow Rotom

How to Say It: ROW-tom
Imperial Height: 1'
Metric Height: 0.3 m
Imperial Weight: 0.7 lbs.
Metric Weight: 0.3 kg
Gender: Unknown
Ability: Levitate
Weaknesses: Ghost, Dark

POKÉMON SWORD:
One boy's invention led to the development of many different machines that take advantage of Rotom's unique capabilities.

POKÉMON SHIELD:
With a body made of plasma, it can inhabit all sorts of machines. It loves to surprise others.

Does not evolve.

Rufflet
Eaglet Pokémon

How to Say It: RUF-lit
Imperial Height: 1'8"
Metric Height: 0.5 m
Imperial Weight: 23.1 lbs.
Metric Weight: 10.5 kg
Gender: ♂
Ability: Keen Eye / Sheer Force
Weaknesses: Electric, Ice, Rock

POKÉMON SWORD:
If it spies a strong Pokémon, Rufflet can't resist challenging it to a battle. But if Rufflet loses, it starts bawling.

POKÉMON SHIELD:
A combative Pokémon, it's ready to pick a fight with anyone. It has talons that can crush hard berries.

Rufflet ⇨ **Braviary**

Runerigus
Grudge Pokémon

TYPE: Ground-Ghost

How to Say It: ROON-uh-REE-gus
Imperial Height: 5'3"
Metric Height: 1.6 m
Imperial Weight: 146.8 lbs.
Metric Weight: 66.6 kg
Gender: ♂ ♀
Ability: Wandering Spirit
Weaknesses: Water, Ghost, Grass, Dark, Ice

POKÉMON SWORD:
A powerful curse was woven into an ancient painting. After absorbing the spirit of a Yamask, the painting began to move.

POKÉMON SHIELD:
Never touch its shadowlike body, or you'll be shown the horrific memories behind the picture carved into it.

Galarian Yamask ⇨ **Runerigus**

Sableye
Darkness Pokémon

How to Say It: SAY-bull-eye
Imperial Height: 1'8"
Metric Height: 0.5 m
Imperial Weight: 24.3 lbs.
Metric Weight: 11.0 kg
Gender: ♂ ♀
Ability: Keen Eye / Stall
Weaknesses: Fairy

POKÉMON SWORD:
This Pokémon is feared. When its gemstone eyes begin to glow with a sinister shine, it's believed that Sableye will steal people's spirits away.

POKÉMON SHIELD:
It feeds on gemstone crystals. In darkness, its eyes sparkle with the glitter of jewels.

Does not evolve.

TYPE: Poison-Fire

Salandit
Toxic Lixard Pokémon

How to Say It: suh-LAN-dit
Imperial Height: 2'
Metric Height: 0.6 m
Imperial Weight: 10.6 lbs.
Metric Weight: 4.8 kg
Gender: ♂ ♀
Ability: Corrosion
Weaknesses: Water, Psychic, Ground, Rock

POKÉMON SWORD:
Its venom sacs produce a fluid that this Pokémon then heats up with the flame in its tail. This process creates Salandit's poisonous gas.

POKÉMON SHIELD:
This sneaky Pokémon will slink behind its prey and immobilize it with poisonous gas before the prey even realizes Salandit is there.

Salandit ⇨ Salazzle

Salazzle

Toxic Lizard Pokémon

TYPE: Poison-Fire

How to Say It: suh-LAZ-zuhl
Imperial Height: 3'11"
Metric Height: 1.2 m
Imperial Weight: 48.9 lbs.
Metric Weight: 22.2 kg
Gender: ♀
Ability: Corrosion
Weaknesses: Water, Psychic, Ground, Rock

POKÉMON SWORD:
Only female Salazzle exist. They emit a gas laden with pheromones to captivate male Salandit.

POKÉMON SHIELD:
The winner of competitions between Salazzle is decided by which one has the most male Salandit with it.

Salandit ⇨ Salazzle

Sandaconda
Sand Snake Pokémon

How to Say It: san-duh-KAHN-duh
Imperial Height: 12'6"
Metric Height: 3.8 m
Imperial Weight: 144.4 lbs.
Metric Weight: 65.5 kg
Gender: ♂ ♀
Ability: Sand Spit / Shed Skin
Weaknesses: Water, Grass, Ice

POKÉMON SWORD:
When it contracts its body, over 220 pounds of sand sprays from its nose. If it ever runs out of sand, it becomes disheartened.

POKÉMON SHIELD:
Its unique style of coiling allows it to blast sand out of its sand sac more efficiently.

 ⇨

Silicobra   Sandaconda

Gigantamax Sandaconda

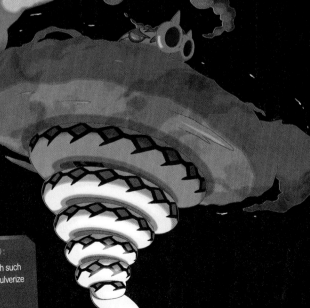

Imperial Height: 72'2"+
Metric Height: 22.0+ m
Imperial Weight: ?????.? lbs.
Metric Weight: ?????.? kg

POKÉMON SWORD:
Its sand pouch has grown to tremendous proportions. More than 1,000,000 tons of sand now swirl around its body.

POKÉMON SHIELD:
Sand swirls around its body with such speed and power that it could pulverize a skyscraper.

Sawk
Karate Pokémon

TYPE:
Fighting

How to Say It: SAWK
Imperial Height: 4'7"
Metric Height: 1.4 m
Imperial Weight: 112. 4 lbs.
Metric Weight: 51.0 kg
Gender: ♂
Ability: Sturdy / Inner Focus
Weaknesses: Flying, Psychic, Fairy

POKÉMON SWORD:
If you see a Sawk training in the mountains in its single-minded pursuit of strength, it's best to quietly pass by.

POKÉMON SHIELD:
The karate chops of a Sawk that's trained itself to the limit can cleave the ocean itself.Does not evolve.

Does not evolve

TYPE:
Fire

Scorbunny
Rabbit Pokémon

How to Say It: SKOHR-buh-nee
Imperial Height: 1'
Metric Height: 0.3 m
Imperial Weight: 9.9 lbs.
Metric Weight: 4.5 kg
Gender: ♂ ♀
Ability: Blaze
Weaknesses: Water, Ground, Rock

POKÉMON SWORD:
A warm-up of running around gets fire energy coursing through this Pokémon's body. Once that happens, it's ready to fight at full power.

POKÉMON SHIELD:
It has special pads on the backs of its feet, and one on its nose. Once it's raring to fight, these pads radiate tremendous heat.

Scorbunny ➡ **Raboot** ➡ **Cinderace**

Scrafty
Hoodlum Pokémon

How to Say It: SKRAF-tee
Imperial Height: 3'7"
Metric Height: 1.1 m
Imperial Weight: 66.1 lbs.
Metric Weight: 30.0 kg
Gender: ♂ ♀
Ability: Shed Skin / Moxie
Weaknesses: Fighting, Flying, Fairy

POKÉMON SWORD:
As halfhearted as this Pokémon's kicks may seem, they pack enough power to shatter Conkeldurr's concrete pillars.

POKÉMON SHIELD:
While mostly known for having the temperament of an aggressive ruffian, this Pokémon takes very good care of its family, friends, and territory.

 ⇨

Scraggy   Scrafty

Scraggy
Shedding Pokémon

How to Say It: SKRAG-ee
Imperial Height: 2'
Metric Height: 0.6 m
Imperial Weight: 26.0 lbs.
Metric Weight: 11.8 kg
Gender: ♂ ♀
Ability: Shed Skin / Moxie
Weaknesses: Fighting, Flying, Fairy

POKÉMON SWORD:
If it locks eyes with you, watch out! Nothing and no one is safe from the reckless headbutts of this troublesome Pokémon.

POKÉMON SHIELD:
It protects itself with its durable skin. It's thought that this Pokémon will evolve once its skin has completely stretched out.

 ⇨

Scraggy   **Scrafty**

Seaking

Goldfish Pokémon

TYPE:
Water

How to Say It: SEE-king
Imperial Height: 4'3"
Metric Height: 1.3 m
Imperial Weight: 86.0 lbs.
Metric Weight: 39.0 kg
Gender: ♂ ♀
Ability: Swift Swim / Water Veil
Weaknesses: Electric, Grass

POKÉMON SWORD:
In autumn, its body becomes more fatty in preparing to propose to a mate. It takes on beautiful colors.

POKÉMON SHIELD:
Using its horn, it bores holes in riverbed boulders, making nests to prevent its eggs from washing away.

Goldeen　⇨　**Seaking**

TYPE:
Grass

Seedot

Acorn Pokémon

How to Say It: SEE-dot
Imperial Height: 1'8"
Metric Height: 0.5 m
Imperial Weight: 8.8 lbs.
Metric Weight: 4.0 kg
Gender: ♂ ♀
Ability: Chlorophyll / Early Bird
Weaknesses: Bug, Fire, Flying, Ice, Poison

POKÉMON SWORD:
If it remains still, it looks just like a real nut. It delights in surprising foraging Pokémon.

POKÉMON SHIELD:
It attaches itself to a tree branch using the top of its head. Strong winds can sometimes make it fall.

Seedot　⇨　**Nuzleaf**　⇨　**Shiftry**

Seismitoad

Vibration Pokémon

How to Say It: SYZ-mih-tohd
Imperial Height: 4'11"
Metric Height: 1.5 m
Imperial Weight: 136.7 lbs.
Metric Weight: 62.0 kg
Gender: ♂ ♀
Ability: Swift Swim / Poison Touch
Weaknesses: Grass

POKÉMON SWORD:
The vibrating of the bumps all over its body causes earthquake-like tremors. Seismitoad and Croagunk are similar species.

POKÉMON SHIELD:
This Pokémon is popular among the elderly, who say the vibrations of its lumps are great for massages.

Tympole   **Palpitoad**   **Seismitoad**

TYPE:
Bug-Ghost

Shedinja

Shed Pokémon

How to Say It: sheh-DIN-ja
Imperial Height: 2'7"
Metric Height: 0.8 m
Imperial Weight: 2.6 lbs.
Metric Weight: 1.2 kg
Gender: Unknown
Ability: Wonder Guard
Weaknesses: Dark, Fire, Flying, Ghost, Rock

Ninjask

Nincada

Shedinja

POKÉMON SWORD:
A most peculiar Pokémon that somehow appears in a Poké Ball when a Nincada evolves.

POKÉMON SHIELD:
A strange Pokémon—it flies without moving its wings, has a hollow shell for a body, and does not breathe.

Shellder

Bivalve Pokémon

How to Say It: SHELL-der
Imperial Height: 1'
Metric Height: 0.3 m
Imperial Weight: 8.8 lbs.
Metric Weight: 4.0 kg
Gender: ♂ ♀
Ability: Shell Armor / Skill Link
Weaknesses: Electric, Grass

POKÉMON SWORD:
It swims facing backward by opening and closing its two-piece shell. It is surprisingly fast.

POKÉMON SHIELD:
Its hard shell repels any kind of attack. It is vulnerable only when its shell is open.

Shellder Cloyster

Shellos

Sea Slug Pokémon

TYPE: Water

West Sea

How to Say It: SHELL-loss
Imperial Height: 1'
Metric Height: 0.3 m
Imperial Weight: 13.9 lbs.
Metric Weight: 6.3 kg
Gender: Unknown
Ability: Sticky Hold / Storm Drain
Weaknesses: Grass, Electric

POKÉMON SWORD:
There's speculation that its appearance is determined by what it eats, but the truth remains elusive.

POKÉMON SHIELD:
Its appearance changes depending on the environment. One theory suggests that living in cold seas causes Shellos to take on this form.

 Shellos Gastrodon

Shelmet
Snail Pokémon

How to Say It: SHELL-meht
Imperial Height: 1'4"
Metric Height: 0.4 m
Imperial Weight: 17.0 lbs.
Metric Weight: 7.7 kg
Gender: ♂ ♀
Ability: Hydration / Shell Armor
Weaknesses: Fire, Flying, Rock

POKÉMON SWORD:
When attacked, it tightly shuts the lid of its shell. This reaction fails to protect it from Karrablast, however, because they can still get into the shell.

POKÉMON SHIELD:
It has a strange physiology that responds to electricity. When together with Karrablast, Shelmet evolves for some reason.

Shelmet **Accelgor**

Shiftry
Wicked Pokémon

TYPE:
Grass-Dark

How to Say It: SHIFT-tree
Imperial Height: 4'3"
Metric Height: 1.3 m
Imperial Weight: 131.4 lbs.
Metric Weight: 59.6 kg
Gender: ♂ ♀
Ability: Chlorophyll / Early Bird
Weaknesses: Bug, Fire, Fighting, Flying, Ice, Poison, Fairy

POKÉMON SWORD:
A Pokémon that was feared as a forest guardian. It can read the foe's mind and take preemptive action.

POKÉMON SHIELD:
It lives quietly in the deep forest. It is said to create chilly winter winds with the fans it holds.

Seedot **Nuzleaf** **Shiftry**

Shiinotic
Illuminating Pokémon

TYPE: Grass-Fairy

How to Say It: shee-NAH-tick
Imperial Height: 3'3"
Metric Height: 1.0 m
Imperial Weight: 25.4 lbs.
Metric Weight: 11.5 kg
Gender: ♂♀
Ability: Illuminate / Effect Spore
Weaknesses: Steel, Fire, Flying, Ice, Poison

POKÉMON SWORD:
Its flickering spores lure in prey and put them to sleep. Once this Pokémon has its prey snoozing, it drains their vitality with its fingertips.

POKÉMON SHIELD:
If you see a light deep in a forest at night, don't go near. Shiinotic will make you fall fast asleep.

 ⇨

Morelull   Shiinotic

TYPE: Bug-Rock

Shuckle
Mold Pokémon

How to Say It: SHUCK-kull
Imperial Height: 2'
Metric Height: 0.6 m
Imperial Weight: 45.2 lbs.
Metric Weight: 20.5 kg
Gender: ♂♀
Ability: Sturdy / Gluttony
Weaknesses: Rock, Steel, Water

POKÉMON SWORD:
It stores berries inside its shell. To avoid attacks, it hides beneath rocks and remains completely still.

POKÉMON SHIELD:
The berries stored in its vaselike shell eventually become a thick, pulpy juice.

Does not evolve.

Sigilyph
Avianoid Pokémon

How to Say It: SIH-jih-liff
Imperial Height: 4'7"
Metric Height: 1.4 m
Imperial Weight: 30.9 lbs.
Metric Weight: 14.0 kg
Gender: ♂ ♀
Ability: Wonder Skin / Magic Guard
Weaknesses: Electric, Ice, Rock, Ghost, Dark

POKÉMON SWORD:
Psychic power allows these Pokémon to fly. Some say they were the guardians of an ancient city. Others say they were the guardians' emissaries.

POKÉMON SHIELD:
A discovery was made in the desert where Sigilyph fly. The ruins of what may have been an ancient city were found beneath the sands.

Does not evolve.

TYPE:
Ground

Silicobra
Sand Snake Pokémon

How to Say It: sih-lih-KOH-bruh
Imperial Height: 7'3"
Metric Height: 2.2 m
Imperial Weight: 16.8 lbs.
Metric Weight: 7.6 kg
Gender: ♂ ♀
Ability: Sand Spit / Shed Skin
Weaknesses: Water, Grass, Ice

POKÉMON SWORD:
As it digs, it swallows sand and stores it in its neck pouch. The pouch can hold more than 17 pounds of sand.

POKÉMON SHIELD:
It spews sand from its nostrils. While the enemy is blinded, it burrows into the ground to hide.

 ➡

Silicobra   **Sandaconda**

Silvally
Synthetic Pokémon

TYPE:
Normal

How to Say It: sill-VAL-lie
Imperial Height: 7'7"
Metric Height: 2.3 m
Imperial Weight: 221.6 lbs.
Metric Weight: 100.5 kg
Gender: Unknown
Ability: RKS System
Weaknesses: Fighting

POKÉMON SWORD:
A solid bond of trust between this Pokémon and its Trainer awakened the strength hidden within Silvally. It can change its type at will.

POKÉMON SHIELD:
The final factor needed to release this Pokémon's true power was a strong bond with a Trainer it trusts.

Type: Null ➡ **Silvally**

Sinistea
Black Tea Pokémon

TYPE:
Ghost

How to Say It: SIH-nis-tee
Imperial Height: 4"
Metric Height: 0.1 m
Imperial Weight: 0.4 lbs.
Metric Weight: 0.2 kg
Gender: ♂♀
Ability: Weak Armor
Weaknesses: Ghost, Dark

POKÉMON SWORD:
This Pokémon is said to have been born when a lonely spirit possessed a cold, leftover cup of tea.

POKÉMON SHIELD:
The teacup in which this Pokémon makes its home is a famous piece of antique tableware. Many forgeries are in circulation.

Sinistea　　Polteageist

Sirfetch'd
Wild Duck Pokémon

TYPE:
Fighting

How to Say It: sir-fehcht
Imperial Height: 2'7"
Metric Height: 0.8 m
Imperial Weight: 257.9 lbs.
Metric Weight: 117.0 kg
Gender: ♂♀
Ability: Steadfast
Weaknesses: Psychic, Flying, Fairy

POKÉMON SWORD:
Only Farfetch'd that have survived many battles can attain this evolution. When this Pokémon's leek withers, it will retire from combat.

POKÉMON SHIELD:
After deflecting attacks with its hard leaf shield, it strikes back with its sharp leek stalk. The leek stalk is both weapon and food.

Galarian
Farfetch'd　　Sirfetch'd

Sizzlipede
Radiator Pokémon

How to Say It: SIZ-lih-peed
Imperial Height: 2'4"
Metric Height: 0.7 m
Imperial Weight: 2.2 lbs.
Metric Weight: 1.0 kg
Gender: ♂ ♀
Ability: Flash Fire / White Smoke
Weaknesses: Water, Flying, Rock

POKÉMON SWORD:
It stores flammable gas in its body and uses it to generate heat. The yellow sections on its belly get particularly hot.

POKÉMON SHIELD:
It wraps prey up with its heated body, cooking them in its coils. Once they're well-done, it will voraciously nibble them down to the last morsel.

Sizzlipede **Centiskorch**

Skorupi
Scorpion Pokémon

TYPE:
Poison-Bug

How to Say It: skor-ROOP-ee
Imperial Height: 2'7"
Metric Height: 0.8 m
Imperial Weight: 26.5 lbs.
Metric Weight: 12.0 kg
Gender: ♂ ♀
Ability: Battle Armor / Sniper
Weaknesses: Fire, Flying, Psychic, Rock

POKÉMON SWORD:
After burrowing into the sand, it waits patiently for prey to come near. This Pokémon and Sizzlipede share common descent.

POKÉMON SHIELD:
It attacks using the claws on its tail. Once locked in its grip, its prey is unable to move as this Pokémon's poison seeps in.

Skorupi **Drapion**

Skuntank

Skunk Pokémon

How to Say It: SKUN-tank
Imperial Height: 3'3"
Metric Height: 1.0 m
Imperial Weight: 83.8 lbs.
Metric Weight: 38.0 kg
Gender: ♂♀
Ability: Stench / Aftermath
Weaknesses: Ground

POKÉMON SWORD:
In its belly, it reserves stinky fluid that it shoots from its tail during battle. As this Pokémon's diet varies, so does the stench of its fluid.

POKÉMON SHIELD:
It digs holes in the ground to make its nest. The stench of the fluid it lets fly from the tip of its tail is extremely potent.

Stunky   **Skuntank**

Skwovet

Cheeky Pokémon

TYPE:
Normal

How to Say It: SKWUH-vet
Imperial Height: 1'
Metric Height: 0.3 m
Imperial Weight: 5.5 lbs.
Metric Weight: 2.5 kg
Gender: ♂♀
Ability: Cheek Pouch
Weaknesses: Fighting

POKÉMON SWORD:
Found throughout the Galar region, this Pokémon becomes uneasy if its cheeks are ever completely empty of berries.

POKÉMON SHIELD:
It eats berries nonstop—a habit that has made it more resilient than it looks. It'll show up on farms, searching for yet more berries.

Skwovet   **Greedent**

Sliggoo
Soft Tissue Pokémon

How to Say It: SLIH-goo
Imperial Height: 2'7"
Metric Height: 0.8 m
Imperial Weight: 38.6 lbs.
Metric Weight: 17.5 kg
Gender: ♂ ♀
Ability: Sap Sipper / Hydration
Weaknesses: Fairy, Ice, Dragon

POKÉMON SWORD:
Although this Pokémon isn't very strong, its body is coated in a caustic slime that can melt through anything, so predators steer clear of it.

POKÉMON SHIELD:
The lump on its back contains its tiny brain. It thinks only of food and escaping its enemies.

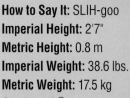

Goomy ⇨ Sliggoo ⇨ Goodra

Slurpuff
Meringue Pokémon

TYPE: Fairy

How to Say It: SLUR-puff
Imperial Height: 2'7"
Metric Height: 0.8 m
Imperial Weight: 11.0 lbs.
Metric Weight: 5.0 kg
Gender: ♂ ♀
Ability: Sweet Veil
Weaknesses: Steel, Poison

POKÉMON SWORD:
By taking in a person's scent, it can sniff out their mental and physical condition. It's hoped that this skill will have many medical applications.

POKÉMON SHIELD:
Slurpuff's fur contains a lot of air, making it soft to the touch and lighter than it looks.

 ⇨

Swirlix   Slurpuff

Sneasel
Sharp Claw Pokémon

How to Say It: SNEE-zul
Imperial Height: 2'11"
Metric Height: 0.9 m
Imperial Weight: 61.7 lbs.
Metric Weight: 28.0 kg
Gender: ♂♀
Ability: Inner Focus / Keen Eye
Weaknesses: Fighting, Bug, Fire, Rock, Steel, Fairy

POKÉMON SWORD:
Its paws conceal sharp claws. If attacked, it suddenly extends the claws and startles its enemy.

POKÉMON SHIELD:
It has a cunning yet savage disposition. It waits for parents to leave their nests, and then it sneaks in to steal their eggs.

Sneasel ➡ Weavile

TYPE:
Ice-Bug

Snom
Worm Pokémon

How to Say It: snahm
Imperial Height: 1'
Metric Height: 0.3 m
Imperial Weight: 8.4 lbs.
Metric Weight: 3.8 kg
Gender: ♂♀
Ability: Shield Dust
Weaknesses: Fire, Steel, Flying, Rock

POKÉMON SWORD:
It spits out thread imbued with a frigid sort of energy and uses it to tie its body to branches, disguising itself as an icicle while it sleeps.

POKÉMON SHIELD:
It eats snow that piles up on the ground. The more snow it eats, the bigger and more impressive the spikes on its back grow.

Snom ➡ Frosmoth

Snorlax
Sleeping Pokémon

TYPE: Normal

How to Say It: SNOR-lacks
Imperial Height: 6'11"
Metric Height: 2.1 m
Imperial Weight: 1014.1 lbs.
Metric Weight: 460.0 kg
Gender: ♂ ♀
Ability: Immunity / Thick Fat
Weaknesses: Fighting

POKÉMON SWORD:
It is not satisfied unless it eats over 880 pounds of food every day. When it is done eating, it goes promptly to sleep.

POKÉMON SHIELD:
This Pokémon's stomach is so strong, even eating moldy or rotten food will not affect it.

Munchlax ⇨ **Snorlax**

Gigantamax Snorlax

Imperial Height: 114'10"+
Metric Height: 35.0 + m
Imperial Weight: ?????.? lbs.
Metric Weight: ?????.? kg

POKÉMON SWORD:
Gigantamax energy has affected stray seeds and even pebbles that got stuck to Snorlax, making them grow to a huge size.

POKÉMON SHIELD:
Terrifyingly strong, this Pokémon is the size of a mountain—and moves about as much as one as well.

Snorunt
Snow Hat Pokémon

TYPE:
Ice

How to Say It: SNOW-runt
Imperial Height: 2'4"
Metric Height: 0.7 m
Imperial Weight: 37.0 lbs.
Metric Weight: 16.8 kg
Gender: ♂ ♀
Ability: Inner Focus / Ice Body
Weaknesses: Fire, Fighting, Rock, Steel

POKÉMON SWORD:
It's said that if they are seen at midnight, they'll cause heavy snow. They eat snow and ice to survive.

POKÉMON SHIELD:
It can only survive in cold areas. It bounces happily around, even in environments as cold as –150 degrees Fahrenheit.

Snorunt

Froslass

Glalie

Snover
Frost Tree Pokémon

TYPE:
Grass-Ice

How to Say It: SNOW-vur
Imperial Height: 3'3"
Metric Height: 1.0 m
Imperial Weight: 111.3 lbs.
Metric Weight: 50.5 kg
Gender: ♂ ♀
Ability: Snow Warning
Weaknesses: Fire, Bug, Fighting, Flying, Poison, Rock, Steel

POKÉMON SWORD:
It lives on snowy mountains. It sinks its legs into the snow to absorb water and keep its own temperature down.

POKÉMON SHIELD:
The berries that grow around its belly are like ice pops. Galarian Darumaka absolutely love these berries.

Snover   Abomasnow

Sobble
Water Lizard Pokémon

How to Say It: SAH-bull
Imperial Height: 1'
Metric Height: 0.3 m
Imperial Weight: 8.8 lbs.
Metric Weight: 4.0 kg
Gender: ♂ ♀
Ability: Torrent
Weaknesses: Grass, Electric

POKÉMON SWORD:
When scared, this Pokémon cries. Its tears pack the chemical punch of 100 onions, and attackers won't be able to resist weeping.

POKÉMON SHIELD:
When it gets wet, its skin changes color, and this Pokémon becomes invisible as if it were camouflaged.

Sobble ⇨ **Drizzile** ⇨ **Inteleon**

Solosis
Cell Pokémon

How to Say It: soh-LOH-sis
Imperial Height: 1'
Metric Height: 0.3 m
Imperial Weight: 2.2 lbs.
Metric Weight: 1.0 kg
Gender: ♂ ♀
Ability: Overcoat / Magic Guard
Weaknesses: Bug, Ghost, Dark

POKÉMON SWORD:
It communicates with others telepathically. Its body is encapsulated in liquid, but if it takes a heavy blow, the liquid will leak out.

POKÉMON SHIELD:
Many say that the special liquid covering this Pokémon's body would allow it to survive in the vacuum of space.

Solosis ⇨ **Duosion** ⇨ **Reuniclus**

Solrock

Meteorite Pokémon

How to Say It: SOLE-rock
Imperial Height: 3'11"
Metric Height: 1.2 m
Imperial Weight: 339.5 lbs.
Metric Weight: 154.0 kg
Gender: Unknown
Ability: Levitate
Weaknesses: Bug, Dark, Ghost, Grass, Steel, Water

POKÉMON SWORD:
When it rotates itself, it gives off light similar to the sun, thus blinding its foes.

POKÉMON SHIELD:
Solar energy is the source of its power, so it is strong during the daytime. When it spins, its body shines.

Does not evolve.

TYPE:
Fairy

Spritzee

Perfume Pokémon

How to Say It: SPRIT-zee
Imperial Height: 8"
Metric Height: 0.2 m
Imperial Weight: 1.1 lbs.
Metric Weight: 0.5 kg
Gender: ♂ ♀
Ability: Healer
Weaknesses: Steel, Poison

POKÉMON SWORD:
A scent pouch within this Pokémon's body allows it to create various scents. A change in its diet will alter the fragrance it produces.

POKÉMON SHIELD:
The scent its body gives off enraptures those who smell it. Noble ladies had no shortage of love for Spritzee.

Spritzee ⇨ Aromatisse

203

Steelix

Iron Snake Pokémon

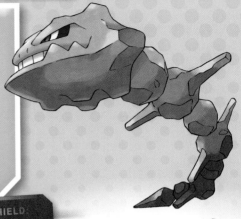

How to Say It: STEE-licks
Imperial Height: 30'2"
Metric Height: 9.2 m
Imperial Weight: 881.8 lbs.
Metric Weight: 400.0 kg
Gender: ♂♀
Ability: Rock Head / Sturdy
Weaknesses: Fighting, Fire, Ground, Water

POKÉMON SWORD:
It is said that if an Onix lives for over 100 years, its composition changes to become diamond-like.

POKÉMON SHIELD:
It is thought its body transformed as a result of iron accumulating internally from swallowing soil.

Onix → Steelix

Steenee

Fruit Pokémon

TYPE: Grass

How to Say It: STEE-nee
Imperial Height: 2'4"
Metric Height: 0.7 m
Imperial Weight: 18.1 lbs.
Metric Weight: 8.2 kg
Gender: ♀
Ability: Leaf Guard / Oblivious
Weaknesses: Fire, Flying, Ice, Poison, Bug

POKÉMON SWORD:
As it twirls like a dancer, a sweet smell spreads out around it. Anyone who inhales the scent will feel a surge of happiness.

POKÉMON SHIELD:
Any Corvisquire that pecks at this Pokémon will be greeted with a smack from its sepals followed by a sharp kick.

Bounsweet → Steenee → Tsareena

Stonjourner

Big Rock Pokémon

TYPE:
Rock

How to Say It: STONE-jer-ner
Imperial Height: 8'2"
Metric Height: 2.5 m
Imperial Weight: 1146.4 lbs.
Metric Weight: 520.0 kg
Gender: ♂ ♀
Ability: Power Spot
Weaknesses: Water, Steel, Grass,
Fighting, Ground

POKÉMON SWORD:
It stands in grasslands, watching the sun's descent from zenith to horizon. This Pokémon has a talent for delivering dynamic kicks.

POKÉMON SHIELD:
Once a year, on a specific date and at a specific time, they gather out of nowhere and form up in a circle.

Does not evolve.

TYPE:
Normal-
Fighting

Stufful

Flailing Pokémon

How to Say It: STUFF-fuhl
Imperial Height: 1'8"
Metric Height: 0.5 m
Imperial Weight: 15.0 lbs.
Metric Weight: 6.8 kg
Gender: ♂ ♀
Ability: Fluffy / Klutz
Weaknesses: Psychic, Flying,
Fairy, Fighting

POKÉMON SWORD:
Its fluffy fur is a delight to pet, but carelessly reaching out to touch this Pokémon could result in painful retaliation.

POKÉMON SHIELD:
The way it protects itself by flailing its arms may be an adorable sight, but stay well away. This is flailing that can snap thick tree trunks.

Stufful ⇨ **Bewear**

GALARIAN
Stunfisk
Trap Pokémon

TYPE:
Ground-
Steel

How to Say It: STUN-fisk
Imperial Height: 2'4"
Metric Height: 0.7 m
Imperial Weight: 45.2 lbs.
Metric Weight: 20.5 kg
Gender: ♂ ♀
Ability: Mimicry
Weaknesses: Fire, Water, Fighting, Ground

POKÉMON SWORD:
Living in mud with a high iron content has given it a strong steel body.

POKÉMON SHIELD:
Its conspicuous lips lure prey in as it lies in wait in the mud. When prey gets close, Stunfisk clamps its jagged steel fins down on them.

Does not evolve.

Stunky
Skunk Pokémon

How to Say It: STUNK-ee
Imperial Height: 1'4"
Metric Height: 0.4 m
Imperial Weight: 42.3 lbs.
Metric Weight: 19.2 kg
Gender: ♂ ♀
Ability: Stench / Aftermath
Weaknesses: Ground

POKÉMON SWORD:
From its rear, it sprays a foul-smelling liquid at opponents. It aims for their faces, and it can hit them from over 16 feet away.

POKÉMON SHIELD:
If it lifts its tail and points its rear at you, beware. It's about to spray you with a fluid stinky enough to make you faint.

Stunky ⇨ **Skuntank**

Sudowoodo
Imitation Pokémon

TYPE: Rock

How to Say It: SOO-doe-WOO-doe
Imperial Height: 3'11"
Metric Height: 1.2 m
Imperial Weight: 83.8 lbs.
Metric Weight: 38.0 kg
Gender: ♂ ♀
Ability: Sturdy / Rock Head
Weaknesses: Fighting, Grass, Ground, Steel, Water

POKÉMON SWORD:
If a tree branch shakes when there is no wind, it's a Sudowoodo, not a tree. It hides from the rain.

POKÉMON SHIELD:
It disguises itself as a tree to avoid attack. It hates water, so it will disappear if it starts raining.

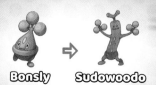

Bonsly ⇨ **Sudowoodo**

Swinub

Pig Pokémon

How to Say It: SWY-nub
Imperial Height: 1'4"
Metric Height: 0.4 m
Imperial Weight: 14.3 lbs.
Metric Weight: 6.5 kg
Gender: ♂ ♀
Ability: Oblivious / Snow Cloak
Weaknesses: Fighting, Fire, Grass, Steel, Water

POKÉMON SWORD:
It rubs its snout on the ground to find and dig up food. It sometimes discovers hot springs.

POKÉMON SHIELD:
If it smells something enticing, it dashes off headlong to find the source of the aroma.

Swinub   Piloswine   Mamoswine

Swirlix

Cotton Candy Pokémon

TYPE:
Fairy

How to Say It: SWUR-licks
Imperial Height: 1'4"
Metric Height: 0.4 m
Imperial Weight: 7.7 lbs.
Metric Weight: 3.5 kg
Gender: ♂ ♀
Ability: Sweet Veil
Weaknesses: Steel, Poison

POKÉMON SWORD:
It eats its own weight in sugar every day. If it doesn't get enough sugar, it becomes incredibly grumpy.

POKÉMON SHIELD:
The sweet smell of cotton candy perfumes Swirlix's fluffy fur. This Pokémon spits out sticky string to tangle up its enemies.

Swirlix   Slurpuff

Swoobat

Courting Pokémon

How to Say It: SWOO-bat
Imperial Height: 2'11"
Metric Height: 0.9 m
Imperial Weight: 23.1 lbs.
Metric Weight: 10.5 kg
Gender: ♂ ♀
Ability: Unaware / Klutz
Weaknesses: Electric, Ice, Rock, Ghost, Dark

POKÉMON SWORD:
Emitting powerful sound waves tires it out. Afterward, it won't be able to fly for a little while.

POKÉMON SHIELD:
The auspicious shape of this Pokémon's nose apparently led some regions to consider Swoobat a symbol of good luck.

Woobat ⇨ Swoobat

TYPE: Fairy

Sylveon

Intertwining Pokémon

How to Say It: SIL-vee-on
Imperial Height: 3'3"
Metric Height: 1.0 m
Imperial Weight: 51.8 lbs.
Metric Weight: 23.5 kg
Gender: ♂ ♀
Ability: Cute Charm
Weaknesses: Steel, Poison

POKÉMON SWORD:
By releasing enmity-erasing waves from its ribbonlike feelers, Sylveon stops any conflict.

POKÉMON SHIELD:
There's a Galarian fairy tale that describes a beautiful Sylveon vanquishing a dreadful dragon Pokémon.

Eevee ⇨ Sylveon

Thievul

Fox Pokémon

TYPE:
Dark

How to Say It: THEEV-ull
Imperial Height: 3'11"
Metric Height: 1.2 m
Imperial Weight: 43.9 lbs.
Metric Weight: 19.9 kg
Gender: ♂ ♀
Ability: Run Away / Unburden
Weaknesses: Fairy, Bug, Fighting

POKÉMON SWORD:
It secretly marks potential targets with a scent. By following the scent, it stalks its targets and steals from them when they least expect it.

POKÉMON SHIELD:
With a lithe body and sharp claws, it goes around stealing food and eggs. Boltund is its natural enemy.

Nickit ⇨ Thievul

Throh

Judo Pokémon

TYPE:
Fighting

How to Say It: THROH
Imperial Height: 4'3"
Metric Height: 1.3 m
Imperial Weight: 122.4 lbs.
Metric Weight: 55.5 kg
Gender: ♂
Ability: Guts / Inner Focus
Weaknesses: Flying, Psychic, Fairy

POKÉMON SWORD:
It performs throwing moves with first-rate skill. Over the course of many battles, Throh's belt grows darker as it absorbs its wearer's sweat.

POKÉMON SHIELD:
They train in groups of five. Any member that can't keep up will discard its belt and leave the group.

Does not evolve.

Thwackey
Beat Pokémon

How to Say It: THWAK-ee
Imperial Height: 2'4"
Metric Height: 0.7 m
Imperial Weight: 30.9 lbs.
Metric Weight: 14.0 kg
Gender: ♂ ♀
Ability: Overgrow
Weaknesses: Fire, Flying, Ice, Poison, Bug

POKÉMON SWORD:
The faster a Thwackey can beat out a rhythm with its two sticks, the more respect it wins from its peers.

POKÉMON SHIELD:
When it's drumming out rapid beats in battle, it gets so caught up in the rhythm that it won't even notice that it's already knocked out its opponent.

Grookey   Thwackey   Rillaboom

Timburr
Muscular Pokémon

TYPE: Fighting

How to Say It: TIM-bur
Imperial Height: 2'
Metric Height: 0.6 m
Imperial Weight: 27.6 lbs.
Metric Weight: 12.5 kg
Gender: ♂ ♀
Ability: Guts / Sheer Force
Weaknesses: Flying, Psychic, Fairy

POKÉMON SWORD:
It loves helping out with construction projects. It loves it so much that if rain causes work to halt, it swings its log around and throws a tantrum.

POKÉMON SHIELD:
Timburr that have started carrying logs that are about three times their size are nearly ready to evolve.

iburr   Gurdurr   Conkeldurr

Togedemaru
Roly-Poly Pokémon

TYPE:
Electric-Steel

How to Say It: TOH-geh-deh-MAH-roo
Imperial Height: 1'
Metric Height: 0.3 m
Imperial Weight: 7.3 lbs.
Metric Weight: 3.3 kg
Gender: ♂♀
Ability: Iron Barbs / Lightning Rod
Weaknesses: Fire, Fighting, Ground

POKÉMON SWORD:
With the long hairs on its back, this Pokémon takes in electricity from other electric Pokémon. It stores what it absorbs in an electric sac.

POKÉMON SHIELD:
When it's in trouble, it curls up into a ball, makes its fur spikes stand on end, and then discharges electricity indiscriminately.

Does not evolve.

TYPE:
Fairy-Flying

Togekiss
Jubilee Pokémon

How to Say It: TOE-geh-kiss
Imperial Height: 4'11"
Metric Height: 1.5 m
Imperial Weight: 83.8 lbs.
Metric Weight: 38.0 kg
Gender: ♂♀
Ability: Hustle / Serene Grace
Weaknesses: Electric, Ice, Rock, Steel, Poison

POKÉMON SWORD:
These Pokémon are never seen anywhere near conflict or turmoil. In recent times, they've hardly been seen at all.

POKÉMON SHIELD:
Known as a bringer of blessings, it's been depicted on good-luck charms since ancient times.

Togepi ⇨ Togetic ⇨ Togekiss

Togepi
Spike Ball Pokémon

TYPE:
Fairy

How to Say It: TOE-ghep-pee
Imperial Height: 1'
Metric Height: 0.3 m
Imperial Weight: 3.3 lbs.
Metric Weight: 1.5 kg
Gender: ♂ ♀
Ability: Hustle / Serene Grace
Weaknesses: Steel / Poison

POKÉMON SWORD:
The shell seems to be filled with joy. It is said that it will share good luck when treated kindly.

POKÉMON SHIELD:
It is considered to be a symbol of good luck. Its shell is said to be filled with happiness.

Togepi   Togetic   Togekiss

TYPE:
Fairy-Flying

Togetic
Happiness Pokémon

How to Say It: TOE-ghet-tic
Imperial Height: 2'
Metric Height: 0.6 m
Imperial Weight: 7.1 lbs.
Metric Weight: 3.2 kg
Gender: ♂ ♀
Ability: Hustle / Serene Grace
Weaknesses: Electric, Ice, Rock, Steel, Poison

POKÉMON SWORD:
They say that it will appear before kindhearted, caring people and shower them with happiness.

POKÉMON SHIELD:
It grows dispirited if it is not with kind people. It can float in midair without moving its wings.

Togepi   Togetic   Togekiss

Torkoal

Coal Pokémon

How to Say It: TOR-coal
Imperial Height: 1'8"
Metric Height: 0.5 m
Imperial Weight: 177.2 lbs.
Metric Weight: 80.4 kg
Gender: ♂♀
Ability: White Smoke / Drought
Weaknesses: Ground, Rock, Water

POKÉMON SWORD:
It burns coal inside its shell for energy. It blows out black soot if it is endangered.

POKÉMON SHIELD:
You find abandoned coal mines full of them. They dig tirelessly in search of coal.

Does not evolve.

Toxapex

Brutal Star Pokémon

TYPE:
Poison-Water

How to Say It: TOX-uh-pex
Imperial Height: 2'4"
Metric Height: 0.7 m
Imperial Weight: 32.0 lbs.
Metric Weight: 14.5 kg
Gender: ♂♀
Ability: Merciless / Limber
Weaknesses: Psychic, Electric, Ground

POKÉMON SWORD:
To survive in the cold waters of Galar, this Pokémon forms a dome with its legs, enclosing its body so it can capture its own body heat.

POKÉMON SHIELD:
Within the poison sac in its body is a poison so toxic that Pokémon as large as Wailord will still be suffering three days after it first takes effect.

Mareanie ⇨ Toxapex

Toxel
Baby Pokémon

How to Say It: TAHKS-ull
Imperial Height: 1'4"
Metric Height: 0.4 m
Imperial Weight: 24.3 lbs.
Metric Weight: 11.0 kg
Gender: ♂♀
Ability: Rattled / Static
Weaknesses: Psychic, Ground

POKÉMON SWORD:
It stores poison in an internal poison sac and secretes that poison through its skin. If you touch this Pokémon, a tingling sensation follows.

POKÉMON SHIELD:
It manipulates the chemical makeup of its poison to produce electricity. The voltage is weak, but it can cause a tingling paralysis.

Toxel ⇨ Toxtricity

TYPE:
Poison-
Fighting

Toxicroak
Toxic Mouth Pokémon

How to Say It: TOX-uh-croak
Imperial Height: 4'3"
Metric Height: 1.3 m
Imperial Weight: 97.9 lbs.
Metric Weight: 44.4 kg
Gender: ♂♀
Ability: Anticipation / Dry Skin
Weaknesses: Psychic, Flying, Ground

POKÉMON SWORD:
It bounces toward opponents and gouges them with poisonous claws. No more than a scratch is needed to knock out its adversaries.

POKÉMON SHIELD:
It booms out a victory croak when its prey goes down in defeat. This Pokémon and Seismitoad are related species.

Croagunk ⇨ Toxicroak

Toxtricity
Punk Pokémon

Low Key Form

How to Say It: tahks-TRIS-ih-tee
Imperial Height: 5'3"
Metric Height: 1.6 m
Imperial Weight: 88.2 lbs.
Metric Weight: 40.0 kg
Gender: ♂ ♀
Ability: Punk Rock / Plus
Weaknesses: Psychic, Ground

POKÉMON SWORD:
When this Pokémon sounds as if it's strumming a guitar, it's actually clawing at the protrusions on its chest to generate electricity.

POKÉMON SHIELD:
This short-tempered and aggressive Pokémon chugs stagnant water to absorb any toxins it might contain.

Toxel

Toxtricity

Tranquill
Wild Pigeon Pokémon

TYPE: Normal-Flying

How to Say It: TRAN-kwill
Imperial Height: 2'
Metric Height: 0.6 m
Imperial Weight: 33.1 lbs.
Metric Weight: 15.0 kg
Gender: ♂♀
Ability: Big Pecks / Super Luck
Weaknesses: Electric, Ice, Rock

POKÉMON SWORD:
It can fly moderately quickly. No matter how far it travels, it can always find its way back to its master and its nest.

POKÉMON SHIELD:
These bright Pokémon have acute memories. Apparently delivery workers often choose them as their partners.

Unfezant (male)

Pidove ⇨ Tranquill ⇨ Unfezant (female)

Trapinch
Ant Pit Pokémon

TYPE: Ground

How to Say It: TRAP-inch
Imperial Height: 2'4"
Metric Height: 0.7 m
Imperial Weight: 33.1 lbs.
Metric Weight: 15.0 kg
Gender: ♂♀
Ability: Hyper Cutter / Arena Trap
Weaknesses: Grass, Ice, Water

POKÉMON SWORD:
Its nest is a sloped, bowl-like pit in the desert. Once something has fallen in, there is no escape.

POKÉMON SHIELD:
It makes an inescapable conical pit and lies in wait at the bottom for prey to come tumbling down.

Trapinch ⇨ Vibrava ⇨ Flygon

Trevenant

Elder Tree Pokémon

TYPE: Ghost-Grass

How to Say It: TREV-uh-nunt
Imperial Height: 4'11"
Metric Height: 1.5 m
Imperial Weight: 156.5 lbs.
Metric Weight: 71.0 kg
Gender: ♂♀
Ability: Natural Cure / Frisk
Weaknesses: Ghost, Fire, Flying, Dark, Ice

POKÉMON SWORD:
People fear it due to a belief that it devours any who try to cut down trees in its forest, but to the Pokémon it shares its woods with, it's kind.

POKÉMON SHIELD:
Small roots that extend from the tips of this Pokémon's feet can tie into the trees of the forest and give Trevenant control over them.

Phantump ⇨ Trevenant

Trubbish

Trash Bag Pokémon

TYPE: Poison

How to Say It: TRUB-bish
Imperial Height: 2'
Metric Height: 0.6 m
Imperial Weight: 68.3 lbs.
Metric Weight: 31.0 kg
Gender: ♂♀
Ability: Stench / Sticky Hold
Weaknesses: Ground, Psychic

POKÉMON SWORD:
Its favorite places are unsanitary ones. If you leave trash lying around, you could even find one of these Pokémon living in your room.

POKÉMON SHIELD:
This Pokémon was born from a bag stuffed with trash. Galarian Weezing relish the fumes belched by Trubbish.

Trubbish ⇨ Garbodor

Tsareena

Fruit Pokémon

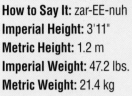

How to Say It: zar-EE-nuh
Imperial Height: 3'11"
Metric Height: 1.2 m
Imperial Weight: 47.2 lbs.
Metric Weight: 21.4 kg
Gender: ♀
Ability: Leaf Guard / Queenly Majesty
Weaknesses: Fire, Flying, Ice,
Poison, Bug

POKÉMON SWORD:
This feared Pokémon has long, slender legs and a cruel heart. It shows no mercy as it stomps on its opponents.

POKÉMON SHIELD:
A kick from the hardened tips of this Pokémon's legs leaves a wound in the opponent's body and soul that will never heal.

Bounsweet Steenee Tsareena

Turtonator

Blast Turtle Pokémon

How to Say It: TURT-nay-ter
Imperial Height: 6'7"
Metric Height: 2.0 m
Imperial Weight: 467.4 lbs.
Metric Weight: 212.0 kg
Gender: ♂ ♀
Ability: Shell Armor
Weaknesses: Ground, Rock, Dragon

POKÉMON SWORD:
Explosive substances coat the shell on its back. Enemies that dare attack it will be blown away by an immense detonation.

POKÉMON SHIELD:
Eating sulfur in its volcanic habitat is what causes explosive compounds to develop in its shell. Its droppings are also dangerously explosive.

Does not evolve.

Tympole
Tadpole Pokémon

How to Say It: TIM-pohl
Imperial Height: 1'8"
Metric Height: 0.5 m
Imperial Weight: 9.9 lbs.
Metric Weight: 4.5 kg
Gender: ♂ ♀
Ability: Swift Swim / Hydration
Weaknesses: Grass, Electric

POKÉMON SWORD:
Graceful ripples running across the water's surface are a sure sign that Tympole are singing in high-pitched voices below.

POKÉMON SHIELD:
It uses sound waves to communicate with others of its kind. People and other Pokémon species can't hear its cries of warning.

Tympole   Palpitoad   Seismitoa

LEGENDARY POKÉMON

Type: Null
Synthetic Pokémon

How to Say It: TYPE NULL
Imperial Height: 6'3"
Metric Height: 1.9 m
Imperial Weight: 265.7 lbs.
Metric Weight: 120.5 kg
Gender: Unknown
Ability: Battle Armor
Weaknesses: Fighting

POKÉMON SWORD:
Rumor has it that the theft of top-secret research notes led to a new instance of this Pokémon being created in the Galar region.

POKÉMON SHIELD:
It was modeled after a mighty Pokémon of myth. The mask placed upon it limits its power in order to keep it under control.

Type: Null   Silvally

Tyranitar
Armor Pokémon

How to Say It: tie-RAN-uh-tar
Imperial Height: 6'7"
Metric Height: 2.0 m
Imperial Weight: 445.3 lbs.
Metric Weight: 202.0 kg
Gender: ♂ ♀
Ability: Sand Stream
Weaknesses: Fighting, Bug, Grass, Ground, Steel, Water, Fairy

POKÉMON SWORD:
Its body can't be harmed by any sort of attack, so it is very eager to make challenges against enemies.

POKÉMON SHIELD:
The quakes caused when it walks make even great mountains crumble and change the surrounding terrain.

Larvitar ⇨ Pupitar ⇨ Tyranitar

Tyrogue
Scuffle Pokémon

TYPE: Fighting

How to Say It: tie-ROHG
Imperial Height: 2'4"
Metric Height: 0.7 m
Imperial Weight: 46.3 lbs.
Metric Weight: 21.0 kg
Gender: ♂
Ability: Guts / Steadfast
Weaknesses: Flying, Psychic, Fairy

POKÉMON SWORD:
It is always bursting with energy. To make itself stronger, it keeps on fighting even if it loses.

POKÉMON SHIELD:
Even though it is small, it can't be ignored because it will slug any handy target without warning.

Hitmonlee

Tyrogue

Hitmonchan

Hitmontop

TYPE: Dark

Umbreon
Moonlight Pokémon

How to Say It: UM-bree-on
Imperial Height: 3'3"
Metric Height: 1.0 m
Imperial Weight: 59.5 lbs.
Metric Weight: 27.0 kg
Gender: ♂ ♀
Ability: Synchronize
Weaknesses: Fighting, Bug, Fairy

POKÉMON SWORD:
When this Pokémon becomes angry, its pores secrete a poisonous sweat, which it sprays at its opponent's eyes.

POKÉMON SHIELD:
On the night of a full moon, or when it gets excited, the ring patterns on its body glow yellow.

Eevee   Umbreon

Unfezant
Proud Pokémon

Female Form

How to Say It: un-FEZ-ant
Imperial Height: 3'11"
Metric Height: 1.2 m
Imperial Weight: 63.9 lbs.
Metric Weight: 29.0 kg
Gender: ♂ ♀
Ability: Big Pecks / Super Luck
Weaknesses: Electric, Ice, Rock

Male Form

FEMALE

POKÉMON SWORD:
Females of this species are very capable fliers, particularly notable for their stamina. They also take longer to adjust to people.

POKÉMON SHIELD:
This Pokémon is intelligent and intensely proud. People will sit up and take notice if you become the Trainer of one.

MALE

POKÉMON SWORD:
Unfezant are exceptional fliers. The females are known for their stamina, while the males outclass them in terms of speed.

POKÉMON SHIELD:
This Pokémon is intelligent and intensely proud. People will sit up and take notice if you become the Trainer of one.

Pidove ➡ Tranquill ➡ Unfezant (male)

➡ Unfezant (female)

Vanillish
Icy Snow Pokémon

TYPE:
Ice

How to Say It: vuh-NIHL-lish
Imperial Height: 3'7"
Metric Height: 1.1 m
Imperial Weight: 90.4 lbs.
Metric Weight: 41.0 kg
Gender: ♂ ♀
Ability: Ice Body / Snow Cloak
Weaknesses: Fire, Fighting, Rock, Steel

POKÉMON SWORD:
By drinking pure water, it grows its icy body. This Pokémon can be hard to find on days with warm, sunny weather.

POKÉMON SHIELD:
It blasts enemies with cold air reaching −148 degrees Fahrenheit, freezing them solid. But it spares their lives afterward—it's a kind Pokémon.

Vanillite Vanillish Vanilluxe

TYPE:
Ice

Vanillite
Fresh Snow Pokémon

How to Say It: vuh-NIHL-lyte
Imperial Height: 1'4"
Metric Height: 0.4 m
Imperial Weight: 12.6 lbs.
Metric Weight: 5.7 kg
Gender: ♂ ♀
Ability: Ice Body / Snow Cloak
Weaknesses: Fire, Fighting, Rock, Steel

POKÉMON SWORD:
Unable to survive in hot areas, it makes itself comfortable by breathing out air cold enough to cause snow. It burrows into the snow to sleep.

POKÉMON SHIELD:
Supposedly, this Pokémon was born from an icicle. It spews out freezing air at −58 degrees Fahrenheit to make itself more comfortable.

Vanillite Vanillish Vanilluxe

Vanilluxe
Snowstorm Pokémon

How to Say It: vuh-NIHL-lux
Imperial Height: 4'3"
Metric Height: 1.3 m
Imperial Weight: 126.8 lbs.
Metric Weight: 57.5 kg
Gender: ♂♀
Ability: Ice Body / Snow Warning
Weaknesses: Fire, Fighting, Rock, Steel

POKÉMON SWORD:
When its anger reaches a breaking point, this Pokémon unleashes a fierce blizzard that freezes every creature around it, be they friend or foe.

POKÉMON SHIELD:
People believe this Pokémon formed when two Vanillish stuck together. Its body temperature is roughly 21 degrees Fahrenheit.

Vanillite ⇨ Vanillish ⇨ Vanilluxe

TYPE: Water

Vaporeon
Bubble Jet Pokémon

How to Say It: vay-POUR-ree-on
Imperial Height: 3'3"
Metric Height: 1.0 m
Imperial Weight: 63.9 lbs.
Metric Weight: 29.0 kg
Gender: ♂♀
Ability: Water Absorb
Weaknesses: Electric, Grass

POKÉMON SWORD:
When Vaporeon's fins begin to vibrate, it is a sign that rain will come within a few hours.

POKÉMON SHIELD:
Its body's cellular structure is similar to the molecular composition of water. It can melt invisibly in water.

 ⇨

Eevee ⇨ Vaporeon

Vespiquen
Beehive Pokémon

How to Say It: VES-pih-kwen
Imperial Height: 3'11"
Metric Height: 1.2 m
Imperial Weight: 84.9 lbs.
Metric Weight: 38.5 kg
Gender: ♀
Ability: Pressure
Weaknesses: Rock, Electric, Fire, Flying, Ice

POKÉMON SWORD:
It skillfully commands its grubs in battles with its enemies. The grubs are willing to risk their lives to defend Vespiquen.

POKÉMON SHIELD:
Vespiquen that give off more pheromones have larger swarms of Combee attendants.

Combee ⇨ Vespiquen

TYPE:
Ground-
Dragon

Vibrava
Vibration Pokémon

How to Say It: vy-BRAH-va
Imperial Height: 3'7"
Metric Height: 1.1 m
Imperial Weight: 33.7 lbs.
Metric Weight: 15.3 kg
Gender: ♂ ♀
Ability: Levitate
Weaknesses: Ice, Dragon, Fairy

POKÉMON SWORD:
The ultrasonic waves it generates by rubbing its two wings together cause severe headaches.

POKÉMON SHIELD:
To help make its wings grow, it dissolves quantities of prey in its digestive juices and guzzles them down every day.

Trapinch ⇨ Vibrava ⇨ Flygon

Vikavolt
Stag Beetle Pokémon

TYPE:
Bug-Electric

How to Say It: VIE-kuh-volt
Imperial Height: 4'11"
Metric Height: 1.5 m
Imperial Weight: 99.2 lbs.
Metric Weight: 45.0 kg
Gender: ♂ ♀
Ability: Levitate
Weaknesses: Fire, Rock

POKÉMON SWORD:
It builds up electricity in its abdomen, focuses it through its jaws, and then fires the electricity off in concentrated beams.

POKÉMON SHIELD:
If it carries a Charjabug to use as a spare battery, a flying Vikavolt can rapidly fire high-powered beams of electricity.

Grubbin   Charjabug   Vikavolt

TYPE:
Grass-Poison

Vileplume
Flower Pokémon

How to Say It: VILE-ploom
Imperial Height: 3'11"
Metric Height: 1.2 m
Imperial Weight: 41.0 lbs.
Metric Weight: 18.6 kg
Gender: ♂ ♀
Ability: Chlorophyll
Weaknesses: Fire, Flying, Ice, Psychic

POKÉMON SWORD:
It has the world's largest petals. With every step, the petals shake out heavy clouds of toxic pollen.

POKÉMON SHIELD:
The larger its petals, the more toxic pollen it contains. Its big head is heavy and hard to hold up.

Vileplume

Oddish   Gloom

Bellossom

Vullaby
Diapered Pokémon

How to Say It: VUL-luh-bye
Imperial Height: 1'8"
Metric Height: 0.5 m
Imperial Weight: 19.8 lbs.
Metric Weight: 9.0 kg
Gender: ♀
Ability: Big Pecks / Overcoat
Weaknesses: Electric, Ice, Rock, Fairy

POKÉMON SWORD:
It wears a bone to protect its rear. It often squabbles with others of its kind over particularly comfy bones.

POKÉMON SHIELD:
Vullaby grow quickly. Bones that have gotten too small for older Vullaby to wear often get passed down to younger ones in the nest.

Vullaby ⇨ **Mandibuzz**

Vulpix
Fox Pokémon

TYPE:
Fire

How to Say It: VULL-picks
Imperial Height: 2'
Metric Height: 0.6 m
Imperial Weight: 21.8 lbs.
Metric Weight: 9.9 kg
Gender: ♂ ♀
Ability: Flash Fire
Weaknesses: Ground, Rock, Water

POKÉMON SWORD:
While young, it has six gorgeous tails. When it grows, several new tails are sprouted.

POKÉMON SHIELD:
As each tail grows, its fur becomes more lustrous. When held, it feels slightly warm.

Vulpix ⇨ **Ninetales**

Wailmer
Ball Whale Pokémon

TYPE: Water

How to Say It: WAIL-murr
Imperial Height: 6'7"
Metric Height: 2.0 m
Imperial Weight: 286.6 lbs.
Metric Weight: 130.0 kg
Gender: ♂ ♀
Ability: Water Veil / Oblivious
Weaknesses: Electric, Grass

POKÉMON SWORD:
It shows off by spraying jets of seawater from the nostrils above its eyes. It eats a solid ton of Wishiwashi every day.

POKÉMON SHIELD:
When it sucks in a large volume of seawater, it becomes like a big, bouncy ball. It eats a ton of food daily.

Wailmer   Wailord

TYPE: Water

Wailord
Float Whale Pokémon

How to Say It: WAIL-ord
Imperial Height: 47'7"
Metric Height: 14.5 m
Imperial Weight: 877.4 lbs.
Metric Weight: 398.0 kg
Gender: ♂ ♀
Ability: Water Veil / Oblivious
Weaknesses: Electric, Grass

POKÉMON SWORD:
It can sometimes knock out opponents with the shock created by breaching and crashing its big body onto the water.

POKÉMON SHIELD:
Its immense size is the reason for its popularity. Wailord watching is a favorite sightseeing activity in various parts of the world.

Wailmer   Wailord

Weavile

Sharp Claw Pokémon

TYPE:
Dark-Ice

How to Say It: WEE-vile
Imperial Height: 3'7"
Metric Height: 1.1 m
Imperial Weight: 75.0 lbs.
Metric Weight: 34.0 kg
Gender: ♂ ♀
Ability: Pressure
Weaknesses: Fighting, Bug, Fire, Rock, Steel, Fairy

POKÉMON SWORD:
They attack their quarry in packs. Prey as large as Mamoswine easily fall to the teamwork of a group of Weavile.

POKÉMON SHIELD:
With its claws, it leaves behind signs for its friends to find. The number of distinct signs is said to be over 500.

Sneasel   **Weavile**

GALARIAN
Weezing

Poison Gas Pokémon

TYPE:
Poison-Fairy

How to Say It: WEEZ-ing
Imperial Height: 9'10"
Metric Height: 3.0 m
Imperial Weight: 35.3 lbs.
Metric Weight: 16.0 kg
Gender: ♂ ♀
Ability: Levitate / Neutralizing Gas
Weaknesses: Steel, Psychic, Ground

POKÉMON SWORD:
This Pokémon consumes particles that contaminate the air. Instead of leaving droppings, it expels clean air.

POKÉMON SHIELD:
Long ago, during a time when droves of factories fouled the air with pollution, Weezing changed into this form for some reason.

Koffing   **Galarian Weezing**

Whimsicott

Windveiled Pokémon

How to Say It: WHIM-sih-kot
Imperial Height: 2'4"
Metric Height: 0.7 m
Imperial Weight: 14.6 lbs.
Metric Weight: 6.6 kg
Gender: ♂ ♀
Ability: Prankster / Infiltrator
Weaknesses: Fire, Ice, Poison,
Flying, Steel

POKÉMON SWORD:
It scatters cotton all over the place as a prank. If it gets wet, it'll become too heavy to move and have no choice but to answer for its mischief.

POKÉMON SHIELD:
As long as this Pokémon bathes in sunlight, its cotton keeps growing. If too much cotton fluff builds up, Whimsicott tears it off and scatters it.

Cottonee **Whimsicott**

Whiscash

Whiskers Pokémon

How to Say It: WISS-cash
Imperial Height: 2'11"
Metric Height: 0.9 m
Imperial Weight: 52.0 lbs.
Metric Weight: 23.6 kg
Gender: ♂ ♀
Ability: Oblivious / Anticipation
Weaknesses: Grass

POKÉMON SWORD:
It makes its nest at the bottom of swamps. It will eat anything—if it is alive, Whiscash will eat it.

POKÉMON SHIELD:
It claims a large swamp to itself. If a foe comes near it, it sets off tremors by thrashing around.

Barboach **Whiscash**

Wimpod
Turn Tail Pokémon

How to Say It: WIM-pod
Imperial Height: 1'8"
Metric Height: 0.5 m
Imperial Weight: 26.5 lbs.
Metric Weight: 12.0 kg
Gender: ♂ ♀
Ability: Wimp Out
Weaknesses: Flying, Electric, Rock

POKÉMON SWORD:
It's nature's cleaner—it eats anything and everything, including garbage and rotten things. The ground near its nest is always clean.

POKÉMON SHIELD:
Wimpod gather in swarms, constantly on the lookout for danger. They scatter the moment they detect an enemy's presence.

Wimpod   Golisopod

Wingull
Seagull Pokémon

TYPE: Water-Flying

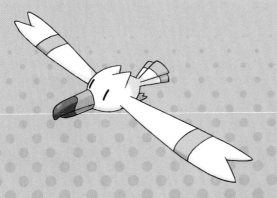

How to Say It: WING-gull
Type: Water-Flying
Imperial Height: 2'
Metric Height: 0.6 m
Imperial Weight: 20.9 lbs.
Metric Weight: 9.5 kg
Gender: ♂ ♀
Ability: Keen Eye / Hydration
Weaknesses: Electric, Rock

POKÉMON SWORD:
It makes its nest on sheer cliffs. Riding the sea breeze, it glides up into the expansive skies.

POKÉMON SHIELD:
It soars on updrafts without flapping its wings. It makes a nest on sheer cliffs at the sea's edge.

Wingull   Pelipper

Wishiwashi
Small Fry Pokémon

How to Say It: WISH-ee-WASH-ee
Imperial Height: 8"
Metric Height: 0.2 m
Imperial Weight: 0.7 lbs.
Metric Weight: 0.3 kg
Gender: ♂ ♀
Ability: Schooling
Weaknesses: Grass, Electric

POKÉMON SWORD:
Individually, they're incredibly weak. It's by gathering up into schools that they're able to confront opponents.

POKÉMON SHIELD:
When it senses danger, its eyes tear up. The sparkle of its tears signals other Wishiwashi to gather.

School Form

Does not evolve.

Wobbuffet
Patient Pokémon

How to Say It: WAH-buf-fet
Imperial Height: 4'3"
Metric Height: 1.3 m
Imperial Weight: 62.8 lbs.
Metric Weight: 28.5 kg
Gender: ♂ ♀
Ability: Shadow Tag
Weaknesses: Bug, Dark, Ghost

POKÉMON SWORD:
It hates light and shock. If attacked, it inflates its body to pump up its counterstrike.

POKÉMON SHIELD:
To keep its pitch-black tail hidden, it lives quietly in the darkness. It is never first to attack.

Wynaut ⇨ **Wobbuffet**

Woobat

Bat Pokémon

How to Say It: WOO-bat
Imperial Height: 1'4"
Metric Height: 0.4 m
Imperial Weight: 4.6 lbs.
Metric Weight: 2.1 kg
Gender: ♂♀
Ability: Unaware / Klutz
Weaknesses: Electric, Ice, Rock, Ghost, Dark

POKÉMON SWORD:
While inside a cave, if you look up and see lots of heart-shaped marks lining the walls, it's evidence that Woobat live there.

POKÉMON SHIELD:
It emits ultrasonic waves as it flutters about, searching for its prey—bug Pokémon.

Woobat → Swoobat

Wooloo

Sheep Pokémon

**TYPE:
Normal**

How to Say It: WOO-loo
Imperial Height: 2'
Metric Height: 0.6 m
Imperial Weight: 13.2 lbs.
Metric Weight: 6.0 kg
Gender: ♂♀
Ability: Fluffy / Run Away
Weaknesses: Fighting

POKÉMON SWORD:
Its curly fleece is such an effective cushion that this Pokémon could fall off a cliff and stand right back up at the bottom, unharmed.

POKÉMON SHIELD:
If its fleece grows too long, Wooloo won't be able to move. Cloth made with the wool of this Pokémon is surprisingly strong.

Wooloo → Dubwool

Wooper
Water Fish Pokémon

TYPE:
Water-Ground

How to Say It: WOOP-pur
Imperial Height: 1'4"
Metric Height: 0.4 m
Imperial Weight: 18.7 lbs.
Metric Weight: 8.5 kg
Gender: ♂♀
Ability: Damp / Water Absorb
Weaknesses: Grass

POKÉMON SWORD:
This Pokémon lives in cold water. It will leave the water to search for food when it gets cold outside.

POKÉMON SHIELD:
When walking on land, it covers its body with a poisonous film that keeps its skin from dehydrating.

Wooper ⇒ **Quagsire**

TYPE:
Psychic

Wynaut
Bright Pokémon

How to Say It: WHY-not
Imperial Height: 2'
Metric Height: 0.6 m
Imperial Weight: 30.9 lbs.
Metric Weight: 14.0 kg
Gender: ♂♀
Ability: Shadow Tag
Weaknesses: Bug, Dark, Ghost

POKÉMON SWORD:
It tends to move in a pack. Individuals squash against one another to toughen their spirits.

POKÉMON SHIELD:
It tends to move in a pack with others. They cluster in a tight group to sleep in a cave.

 ⇒

Wynaut **Wobbuffet**

Xatu
Mystic Pokémon

How to Say It: ZAH-too
Imperial Height: 4'11"
Metric Height: 1.5 m
Imperial Weight: 33.1 lbs.
Metric Weight: 15.0 kg
Gender: ♂♀
Ability: Synchronize / Early Bird
Weaknesses: Dark, Electric, Ghost, Ice, Rock

POKÉMON SWORD:
They say that it stays still and quiet because it is seeing both the past and future at the same time.

POKÉMON SHIELD:
This odd Pokémon can see both the past and the future. It eyes the sun's movement all day.

Natu ⇨ **Xatu**

GALARIAN
Yamask
Spirit Pokémon

How to Say It: YAH-mask
Imperial Height: 1'8"
Metric Height: 0.5 m
Imperial Weight: 3.3 lbs.
Metric Weight: 1.5 kg
Gender: ♂♀
Ability: Wandering Spirit
Weaknesses: Water, Ghost, Grass, Dark, Ice

POKÉMON SWORD:
A clay slab with cursed engravings took possession of a Yamask. The slab is said to be absorbing the Yamask's dark power.

POKÉMON SHIELD:
It's said that this Pokémon was formed when an ancient clay tablet was drawn to a vengeful spirit.

Galarian Yamask ⇨ **Runerigus**

Yamask
Spirit Pokémon

How to Say It: YAH-mask
Imperial Height: 1'8"
Metric Height: 0.5 m
Imperial Weight: 3.3 lbs.
Metric Weight: 1.5 kg
Gender: ♂♀
Ability: Mummy
Weaknesses: Ghost, Dark

POKÉMON SWORD:
It wanders through ruins by night, carrying a mask that's said to have been the face it had when it was still human.

POKÉMON SHIELD:
The spirit of a person from a bygone age became this Pokémon. It rambles through ruins, searching for someone who knows its face.

Yamask ⇨ Cofagrigus

Yamper
Puppy Pokémon

How to Say It: YAM-per
Imperial Height: 1'
Metric Height: 0.3 m
Imperial Weight: 29.8 lbs.
Metric Weight: 13 kg
Gender: ♂♀
Ability: Ball Fetch
Weaknesses: Ground

POKÉMON SWORD:
This Pokémon is very popular as a herding dog in the Galar region. As it runs, it generates electricity from the base of its tail.

POKÉMON SHIELD:
This gluttonous Pokémon only assists people with their work because it wants treats. As it runs, it crackles with electricity.

Yamper ⇨ Boltund

Zacian

Warrior Pokémon

TYPE: Fairy-Steel

How to Say It: ZAH-shee-uhn
Imperial Height: 9'2"
Metric Height: 2.8 m
Imperial Weight: 782.6 lbs.
Metric Weight: 355.0 kg
Gender: Unknown
Ability: Intrepid Sword
Weaknesses: Fire, Ground

POKÉMON SWORD:
Now armed with a weapon it used in ancient times, this Pokémon needs only a single strike to fell even Gigantamax Pokémon.

POKÉMON SHIELD:
Able to cut down anything with a single strike, it became known as the Fairy King's Sword, and it inspired awe in friend and foe alike.

Hero of Many Battles Form

Does not evolve

TYPE: Fighting-Steel

Zamazenta
Warrior Pokémon

Hero of Many Battles Form

How to Say It: ZAH-mah-ZEN-tuh
Imperial Height: 9'6"
Metric Height: 2.9 m
Imperial Weight: 1730.6 lbs.
Metric Weight: 785.0 kg
Gender: Unknown
Ability: Dauntless Shield
Weaknesses: Fire, Fighting, Ground

POKÉMON SWORD:
Its ability to deflect any attack led to it being known as the Fighting Master's Shield. It was feared and respected by all.

POKÉMON SHIELD:
Now that it's equipped with its shield, it can shrug off impressive blows, including the attacks of Dynamax Pokémon.

Does not evolve

GALARIAN
Zigzagoon
Tiny Raccoon Pokémon

TYPE:
Dark-
Normal

How to Say It: ZIG-zag-GOON
Imperial Height: 1'4"
Metric Height: 0.4 m
Imperial Weight: 38.6 lbs.
Metric Weight: 17.5 kg
Gender: ♂ ♀
Ability: Pickup / Gluttony
Weaknesses: Fairy, Bug, Fighting

POKÉMON SWORD:
Its restlessness has it constantly running around. If it sees another Pokémon, it will purposely run into them in order to start a fight.

POKÉMON SHIELD:
Thought to be the oldest form of Zigzagoon, it moves in zigzags and wreaks havoc upon its surroundings.

Galarian   Galarian   Obstagoo
Zigzagoon   Linoone

TYPE:
Dark-
Dragon

Zweilous
Hostile Pokémon

How to Say It: ZVY-lus
Imperial Height: 4'7"
Metric Height: 1.4 m
Imperial Weight: 110.2 lbs.
Metric Weight: 50.0 kg
Gender: ♂ ♀
Ability: Hustle
Weaknesses: Ice, Fighting, Bug, Dragon, Fairy

POKÉMON SWORD:
While hunting for prey, Zweilous wanders its territory, its two heads often bickering over which way to go.

POKÉMON SHIELD:
Their two heads will fight each other over a single piece of food. Zweilous are covered in scars even without battling others.

Deino   Zweilous   Hydreigon